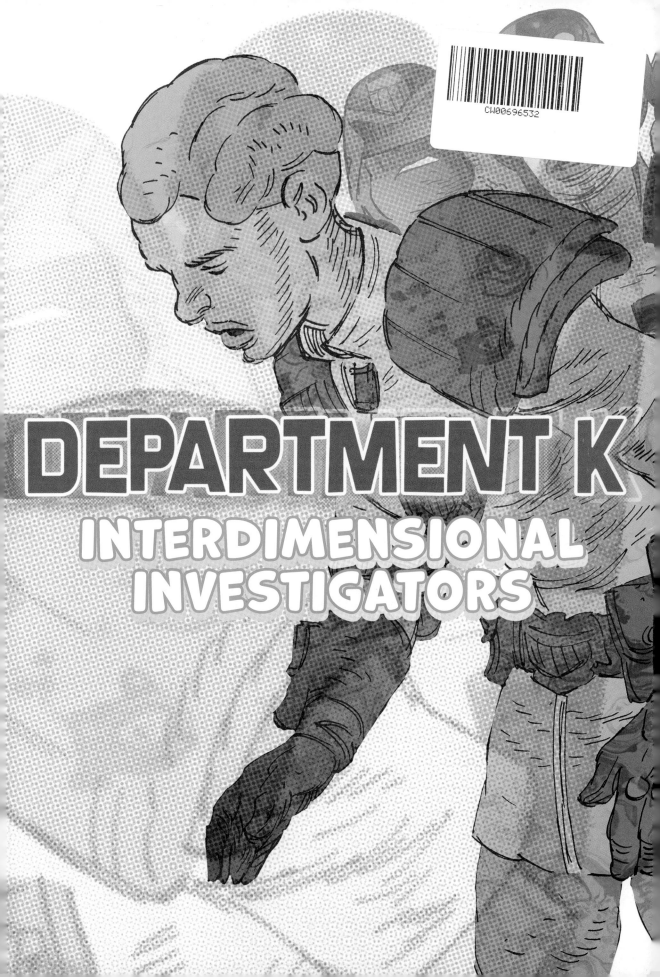

DEPARTMENT K
INTERDIMENSIONAL INVESTIGATORS

DEPARTMENT K

Writer: Rory McConville
Artist: PJ Holden
Colours: Len O'Grady
Letters: Jim Campbell
Originally published in **2000 AD** prog 2196

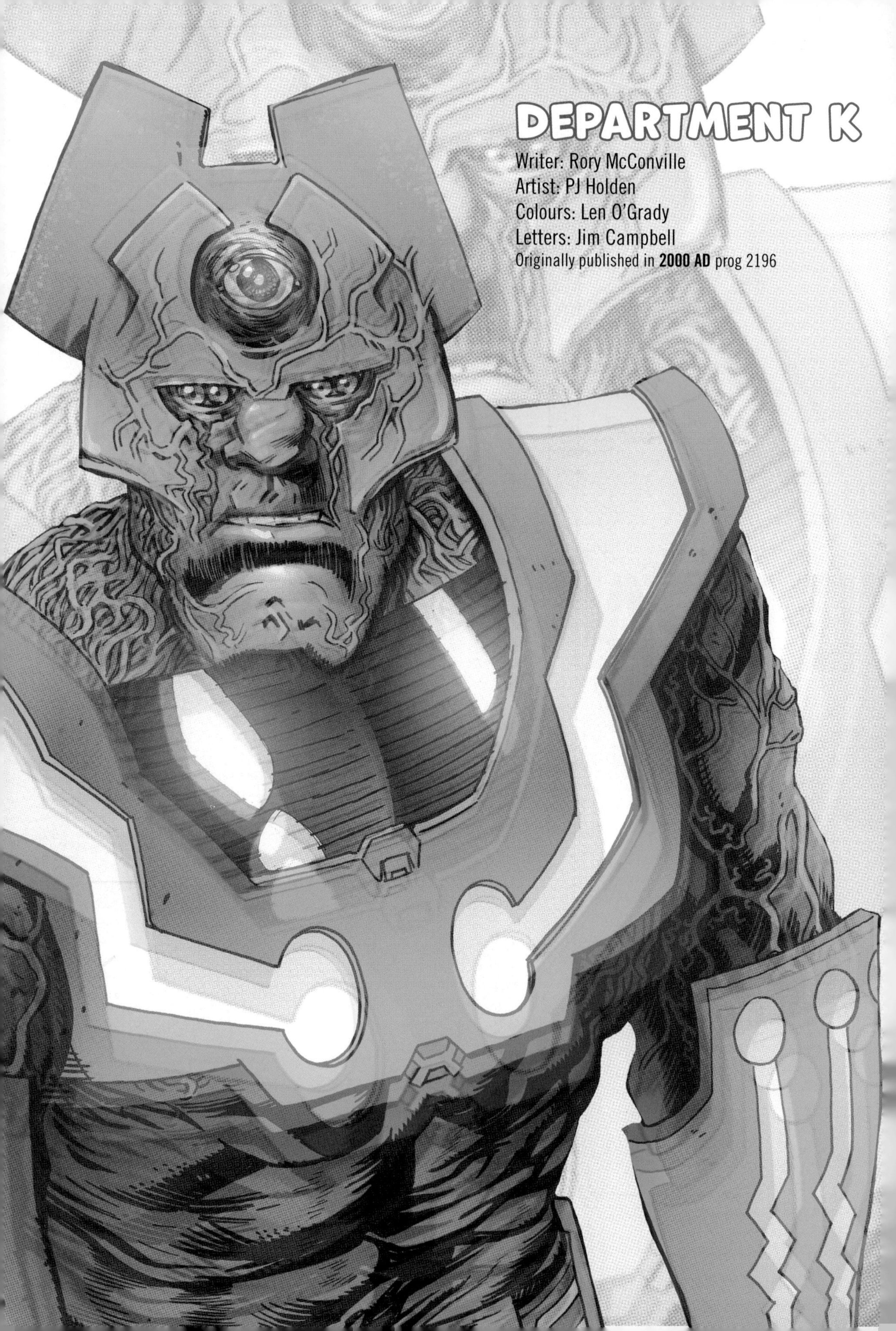

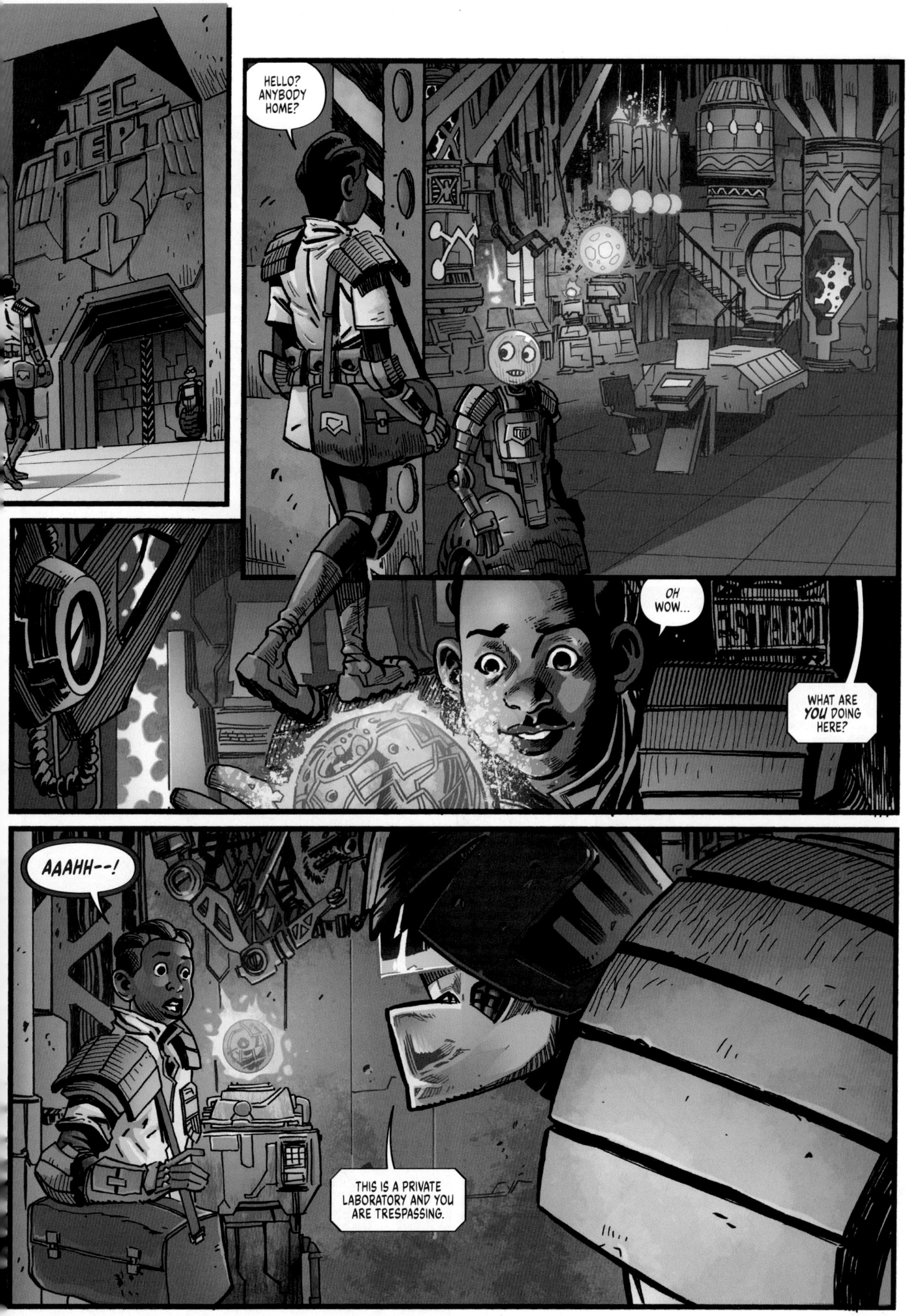
TEC
DEPT
K
HELLO? ANYBODY HOME?
OH WOW...
WHAT ARE YOU DOING HERE?
AAAHH--!
THIS IS A PRIVATE LABORATORY AND YOU ARE TRESPASSING.

WOAH, SORRY. YOU STARTLED ME.

THAT IS JUST A FRACTION OF WHAT WILL HAPPEN TO YOU IF YOU DON'T IDENTIFY YOURSELF IMMEDIATELY.

NAME'S *AFUA*. I'M THE NEW INTERN.

HMM. KIRBY SHOULD'VE BEEN HERE TO MEET YOU BUT, AS USUAL, SHE'S LATE.

I GUESS THAT MEANS I'D BETTER SHOW YOU AROUND.

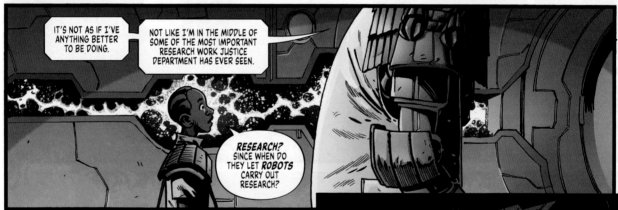

IT'S NOT AS IF I'VE ANYTHING BETTER TO BE DOING.

NOT LIKE I'M IN THE MIDDLE OF SOME OF THE MOST IMPORTANT RESEARCH WORK JUSTICE DEPARTMENT HAS EVER SEEN.

RESEARCH? SINCE WHEN DO THEY LET *ROBOTS* CARRY OUT RESEARCH?

FIRSTLY, I AM *NOT* A ROBOT. SECONDLY--

W-WHAT'S *THAT?*

UGH.

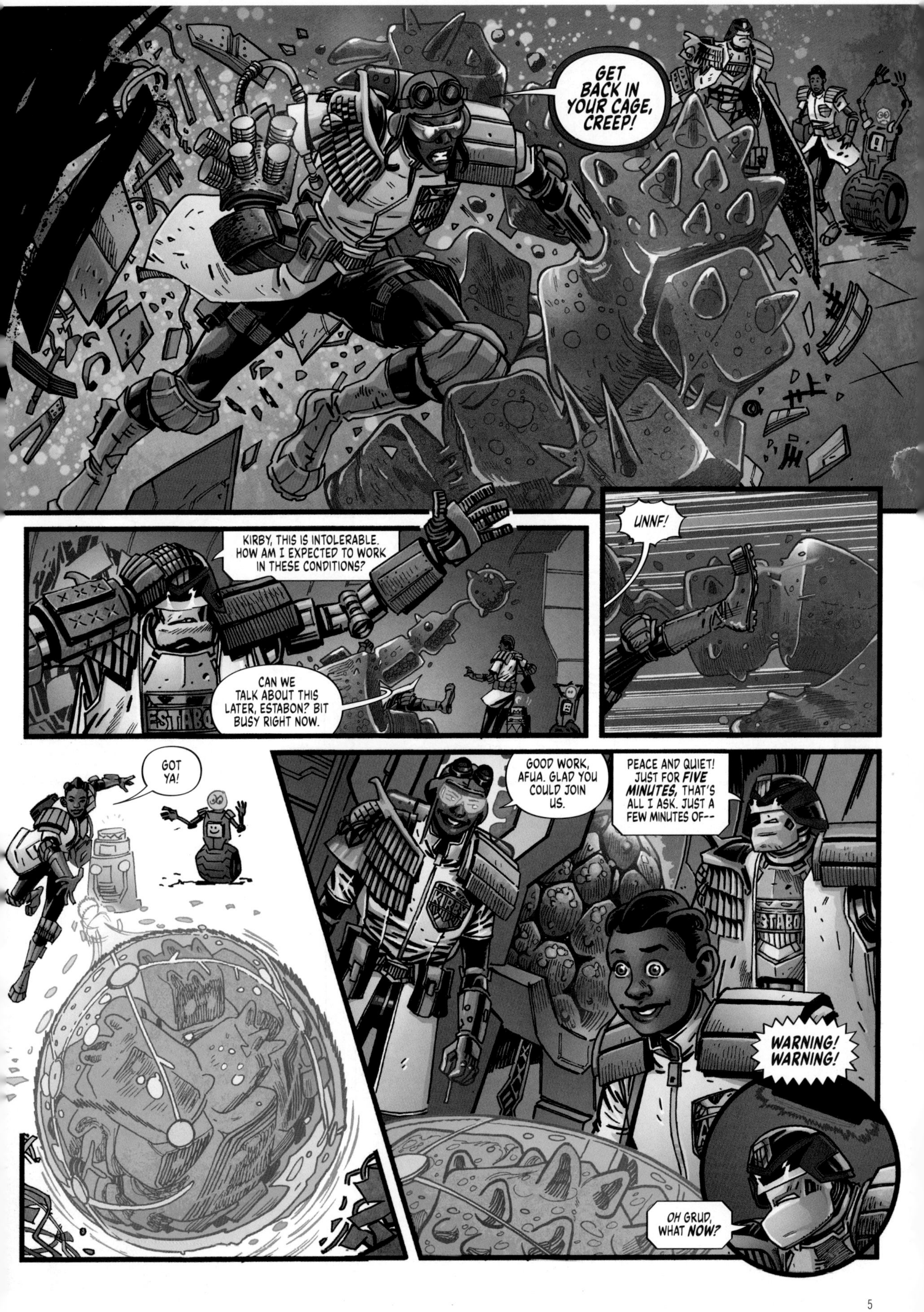
GET BACK IN YOUR CAGE, CREEP!
KIRBY, THIS IS INTOLERABLE. HOW AM I EXPECTED TO WORK IN THESE CONDITIONS?
CAN WE TALK ABOUT THIS LATER, ESTABON? BIT BUSY RIGHT NOW.
UNNF!
GOT YA!
GOOD WORK, AFUA. GLAD YOU COULD JOIN US.
PEACE AND QUIET! JUST FOR FIVE MINUTES, THAT'S ALL I ASK. JUST A FEW MINUTES OF--
WARNING! WARNING!
OH GRUD, WHAT NOW?

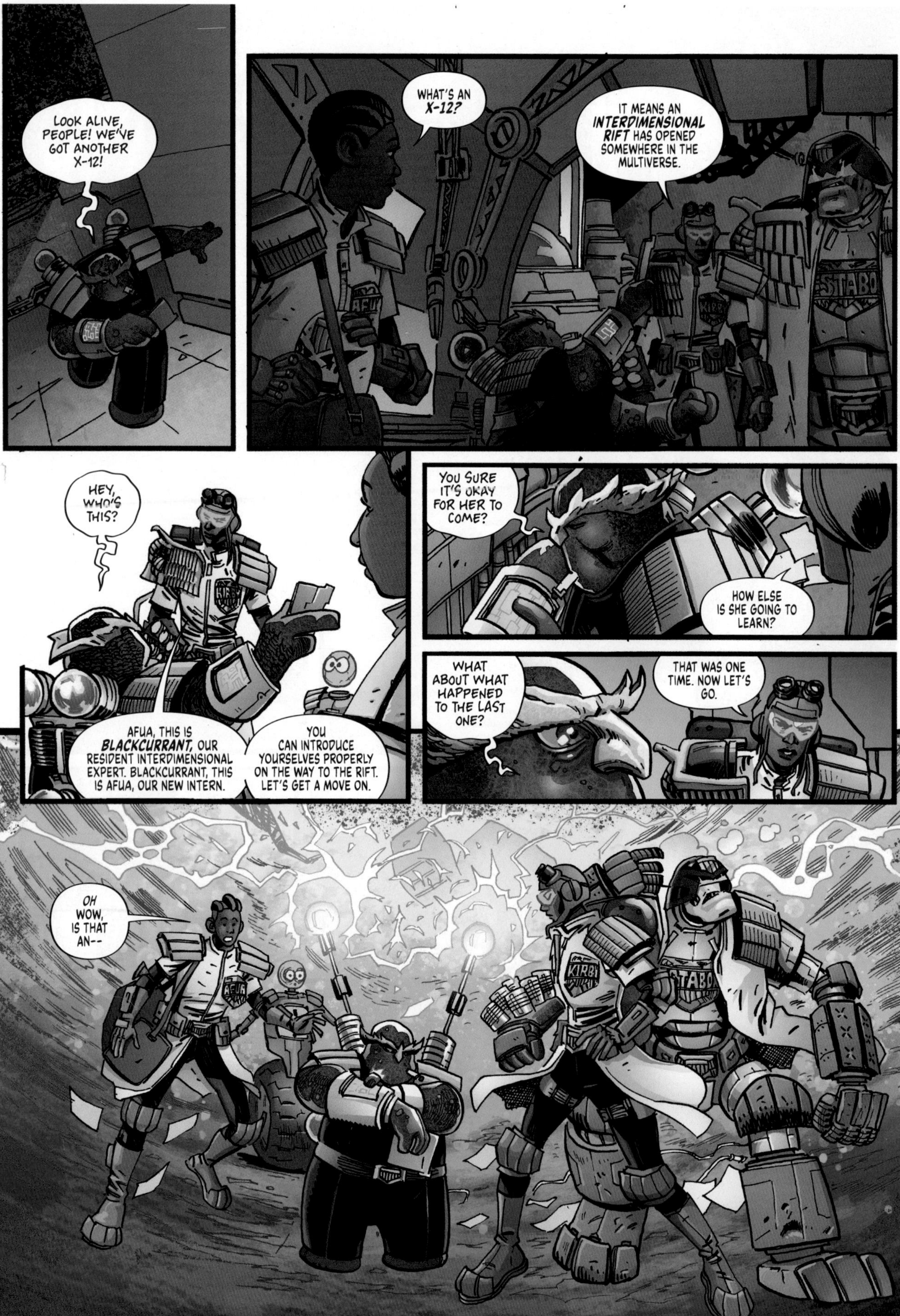
LOOK ALIVE, PEOPLE! WE'VE GOT ANOTHER X-12!
WHAT'S AN X-12?
IT MEANS AN INTERDIMENSIONAL RIFT HAS OPENED SOMEWHERE IN THE MULTIVERSE.
HEY, WHO'S THIS?
AFUA, THIS IS BLACKCURRANT, OUR RESIDENT INTERDIMENSIONAL EXPERT. BLACKCURRANT, THIS IS AFUA, OUR NEW INTERN.
YOU CAN INTRODUCE YOURSELVES PROPERLY ON THE WAY TO THE RIFT. LET'S GET A MOVE ON.
YOU SURE IT'S OKAY FOR HER TO COME?
HOW ELSE IS SHE GOING TO LEARN?
WHAT ABOUT WHAT HAPPENED TO THE LAST ONE?
THAT WAS ONE TIME. NOW LET'S GO.
OH WOW, IS THAT AN--

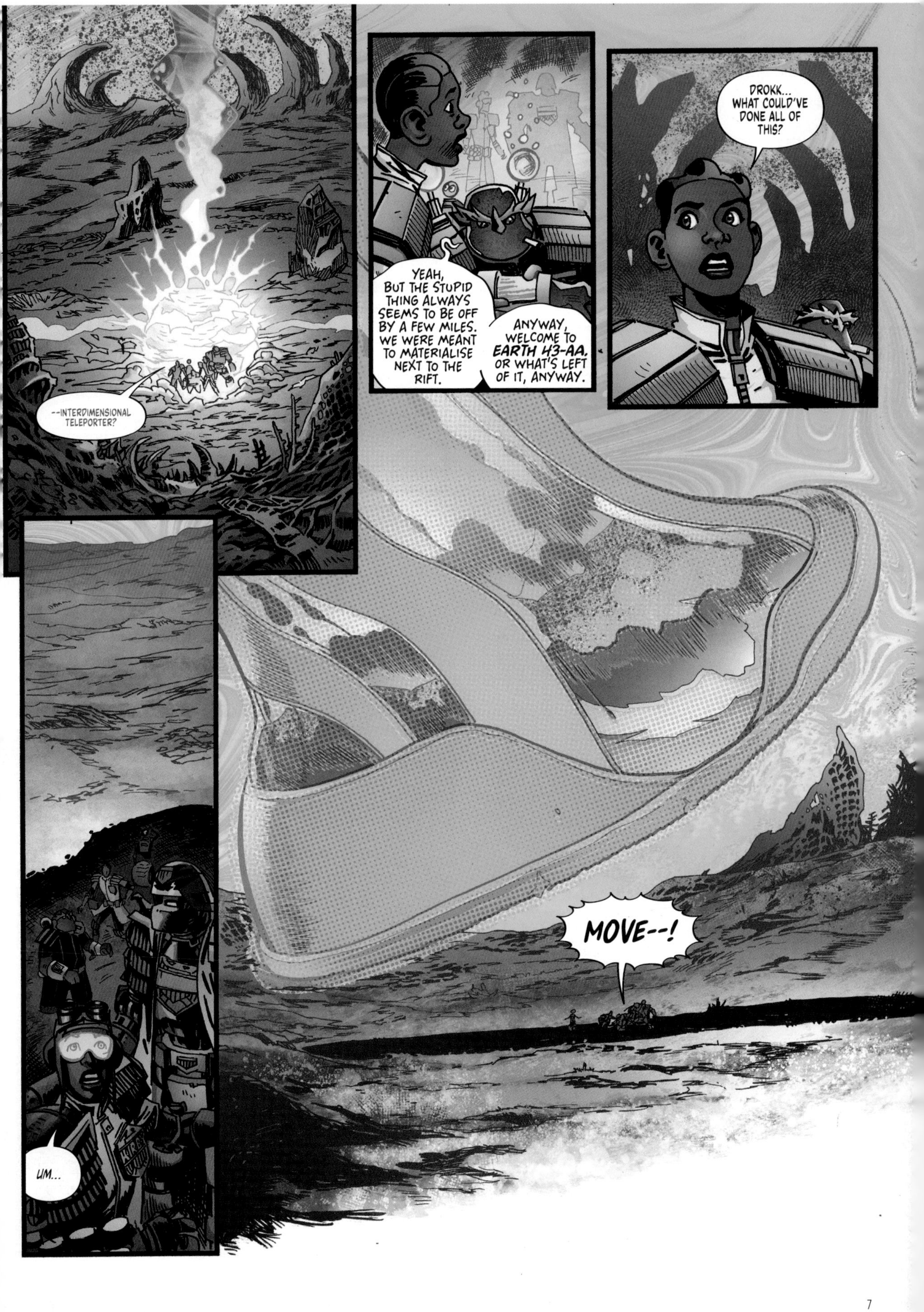
--INTERDIMENSIONAL TELEPORTER?
YEAH, BUT THE STUPID THING ALWAYS SEEMS TO BE OFF BY A FEW MILES. WE WERE MEANT TO MATERIALISE NEXT TO THE RIFT.
ANYWAY, WELCOME TO EARTH 43-AA, OR WHAT'S LEFT OF IT, ANYWAY.
DROKK... WHAT COULD'VE DONE ALL OF THIS?
UM...
MOVE--!

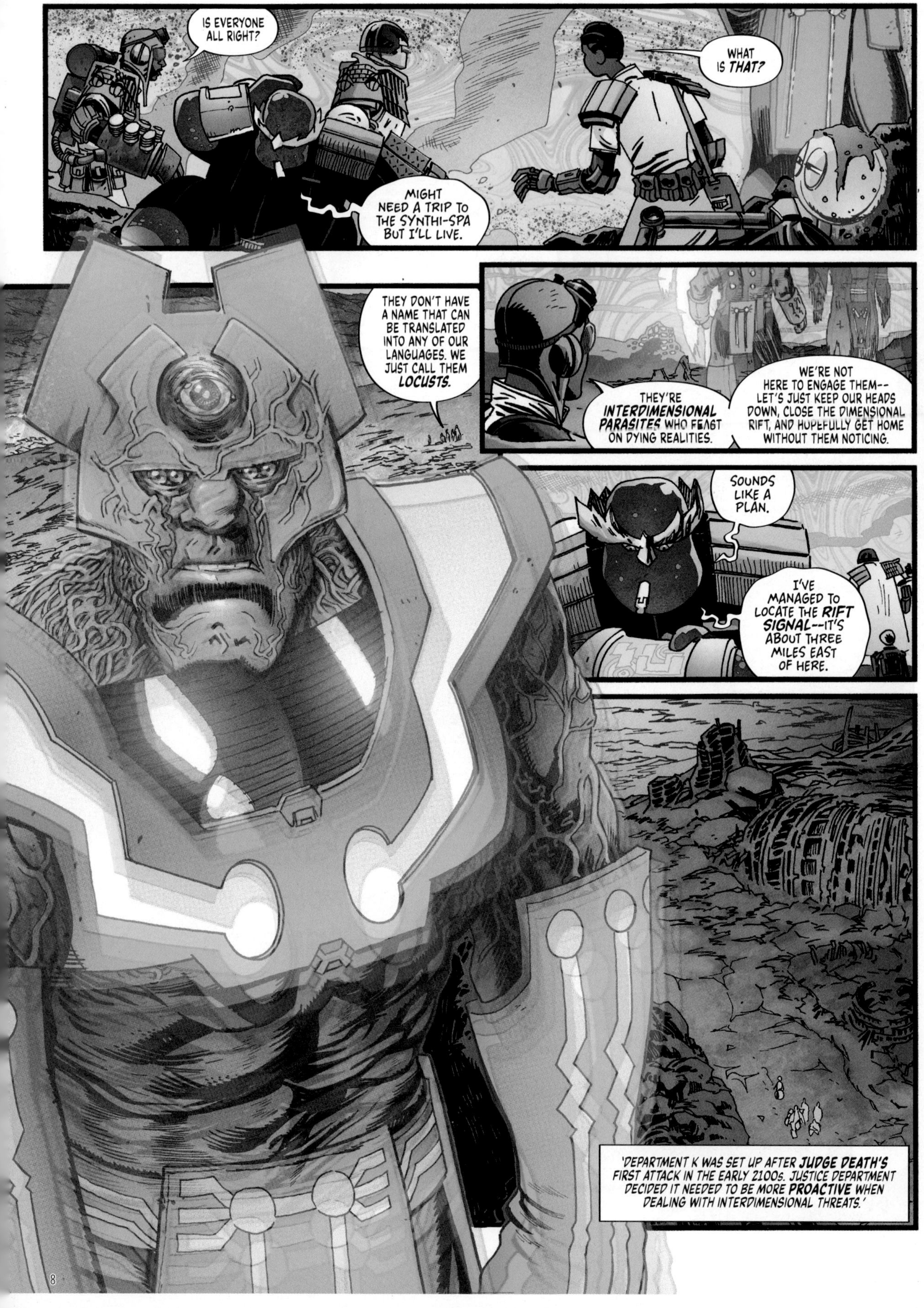

IS EVERYONE ALL RIGHT?
WHAT IS THAT?
MIGHT NEED A TRIP TO THE SYNTHI-SPA BUT I'LL LIVE.
THEY DON'T HAVE A NAME THAT CAN BE TRANSLATED INTO ANY OF OUR LANGUAGES. WE JUST CALL THEM LOCUSTS.
THEY'RE INTERDIMENSIONAL PARASITES WHO FEAST ON DYING REALITIES.
WE'RE NOT HERE TO ENGAGE THEM--LET'S JUST KEEP OUR HEADS DOWN, CLOSE THE DIMENSIONAL RIFT, AND HOPEFULLY GET HOME WITHOUT THEM NOTICING.
SOUNDS LIKE A PLAN.
I'VE MANAGED TO LOCATE THE RIFT SIGNAL--IT'S ABOUT THREE MILES EAST OF HERE.
'DEPARTMENT K WAS SET UP AFTER JUDGE DEATH'S FIRST ATTACK IN THE EARLY 2100s. JUSTICE DEPARTMENT DECIDED IT NEEDED TO BE MORE PROACTIVE WHEN DEALING WITH INTERDIMENSIONAL THREATS.'

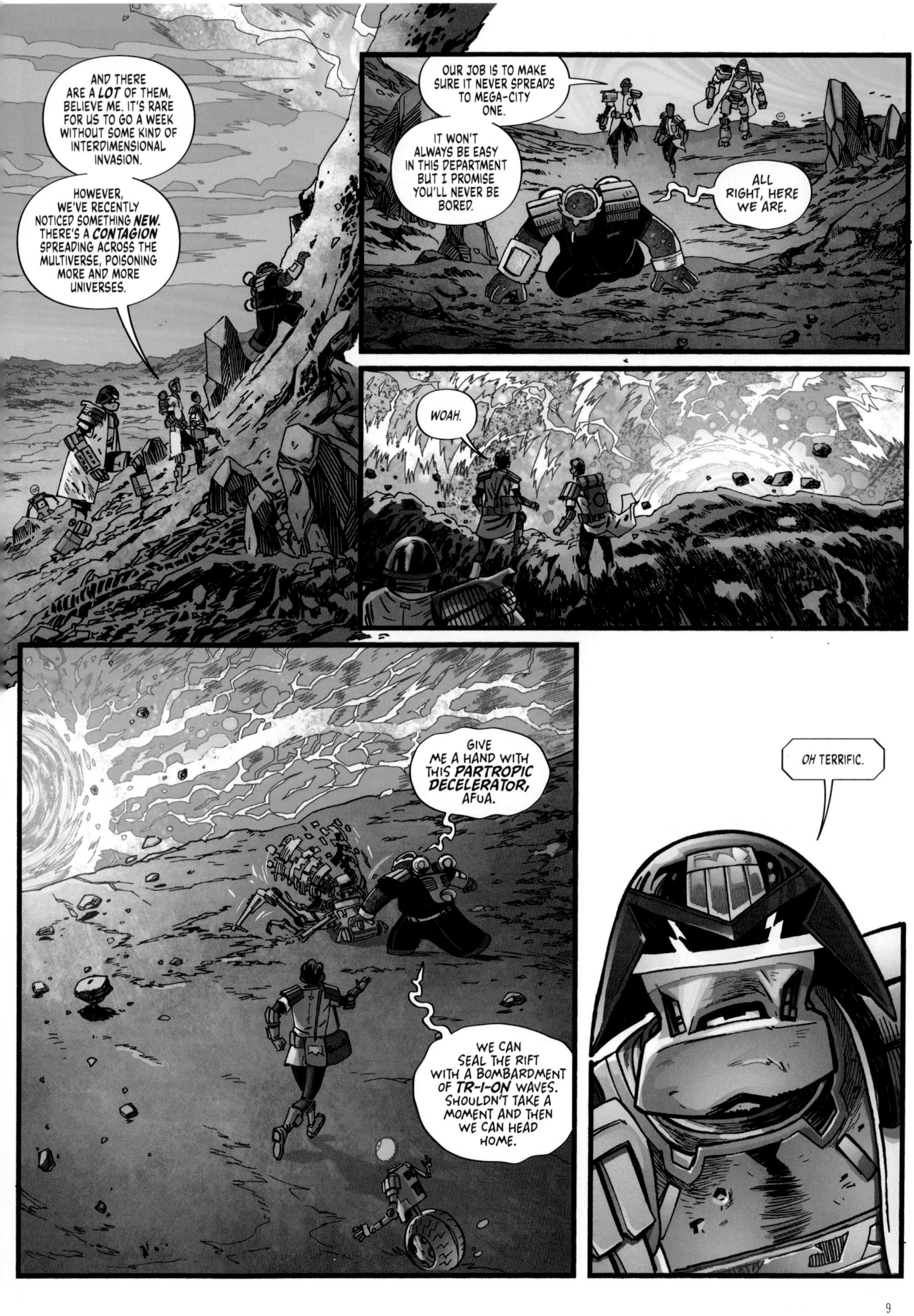
AND THERE ARE A LOT OF THEM, BELIEVE ME. IT'S RARE FOR US TO GO A WEEK WITHOUT SOME KIND OF INTERDIMENSIONAL INVASION.
HOWEVER, WE'VE RECENTLY NOTICED SOMETHING NEW. THERE'S A CONTAGION SPREADING ACROSS THE MULTIVERSE, POISONING MORE AND MORE UNIVERSES.
OUR JOB IS TO MAKE SURE IT NEVER SPREADS TO MEGA-CITY ONE.
IT WON'T ALWAYS BE EASY IN THIS DEPARTMENT BUT I PROMISE YOU'LL NEVER BE BORED.
ALL RIGHT, HERE WE ARE.
WOAH.
GIVE ME A HAND WITH THIS PARTROPIC DECELERATOR, AFUA.
WE CAN SEAL THE RIFT WITH A BOMBARDMENT OF TR-I-ON WAVES. SHOULDN'T TAKE A MOMENT AND THEN WE CAN HEAD HOME.
OH TERRIFIC.

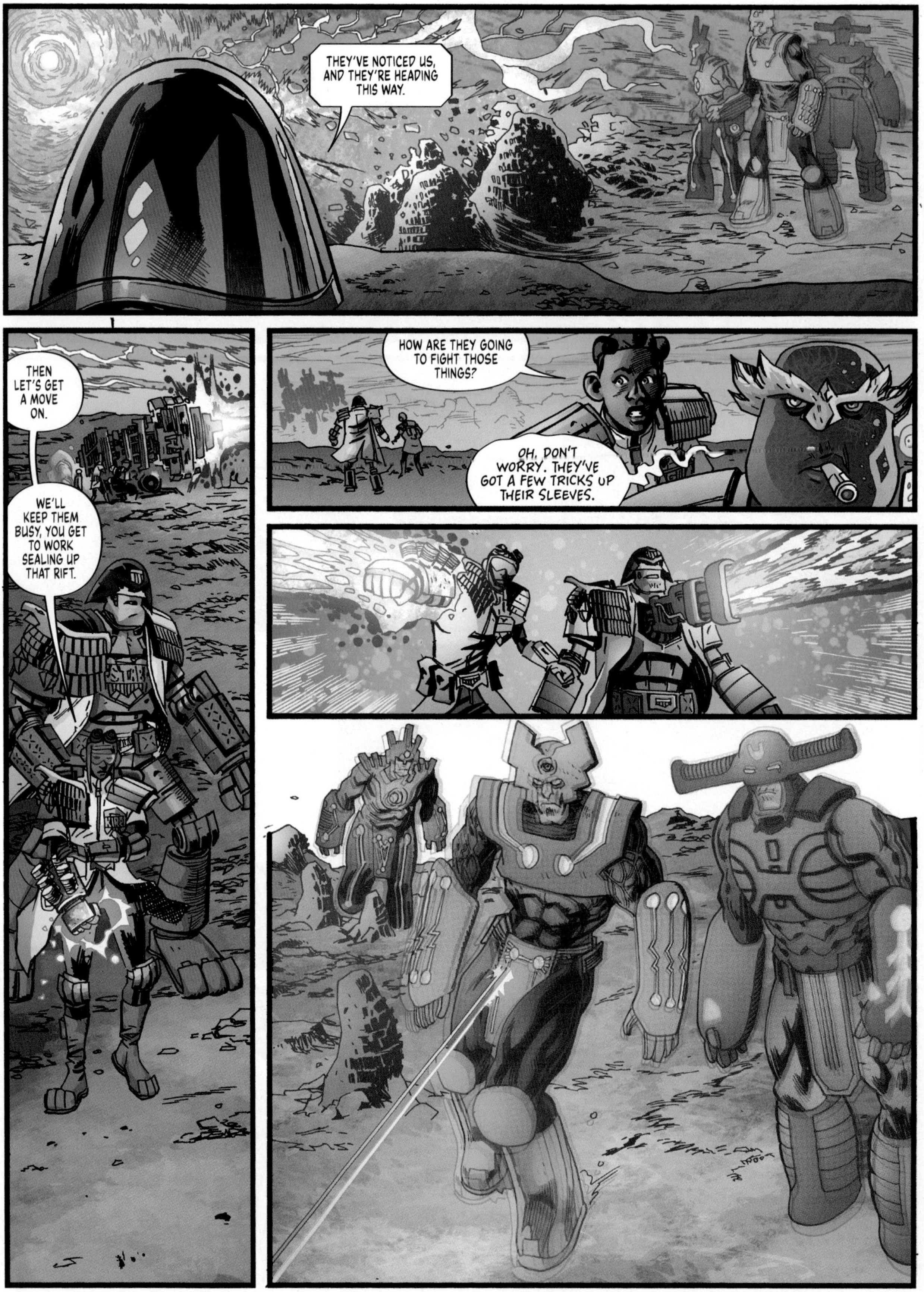
THEY'VE NOTICED US, AND THEY'RE HEADING THIS WAY.
THEN LET'S GET A MOVE ON.
WE'LL KEEP THEM BUSY, YOU GET TO WORK SEALING UP THAT RIFT.
HOW ARE THEY GOING TO FIGHT THOSE THINGS?
OH, DON'T WORRY. THEY'VE GOT A FEW TRICKS UP THEIR SLEEVES.

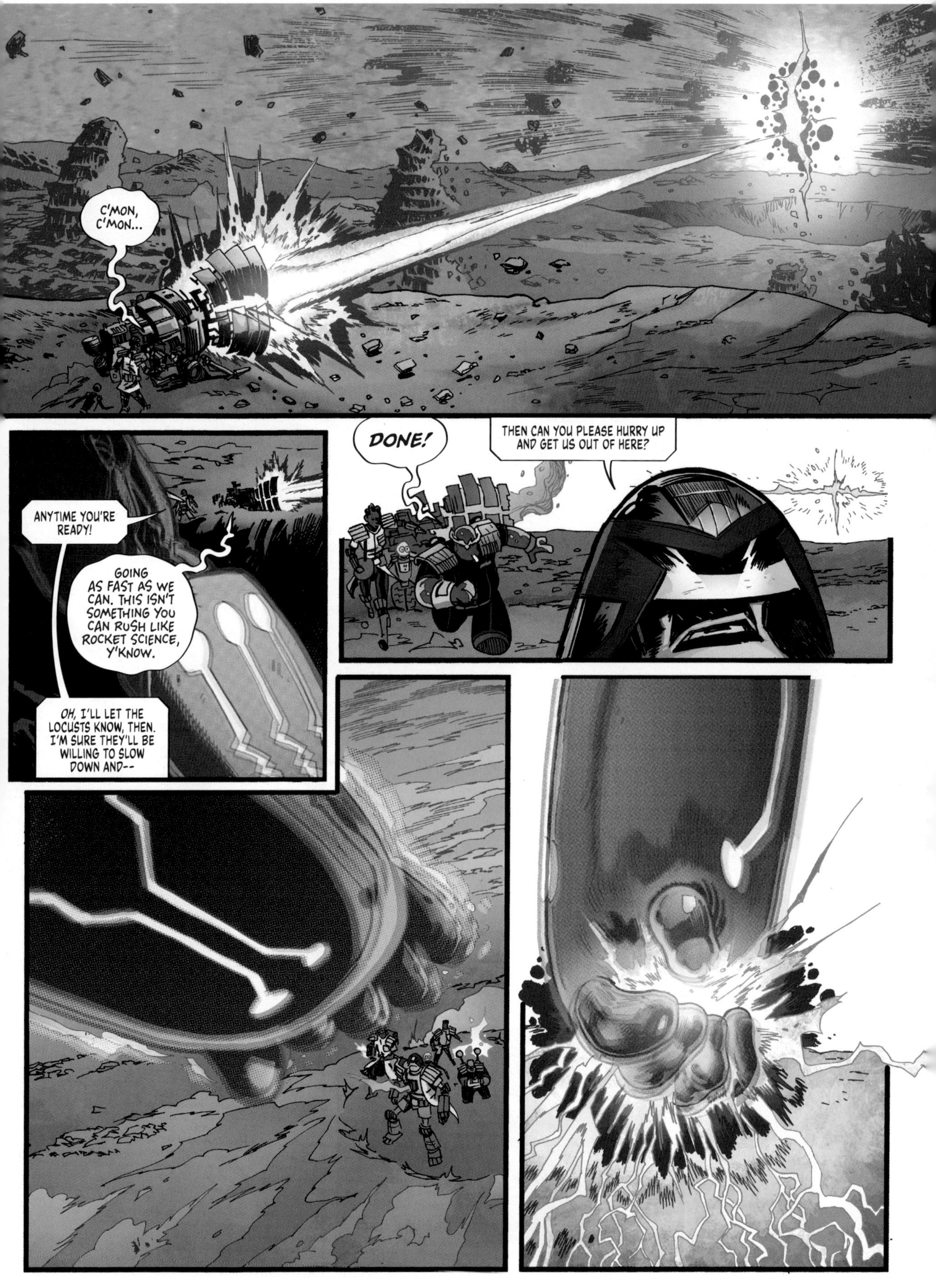
C'MON, C'MON...
ANYTIME YOU'RE READY!
GOING AS FAST AS WE CAN. THIS ISN'T SOMETHING YOU CAN RUSH LIKE ROCKET SCIENCE, Y'KNOW.
OH, I'LL LET THE LOCUSTS KNOW, THEN. I'M SURE THEY'LL BE WILLING TO SLOW DOWN AND--
DONE!
THEN CAN YOU PLEASE HURRY UP AND GET US OUT OF HERE?

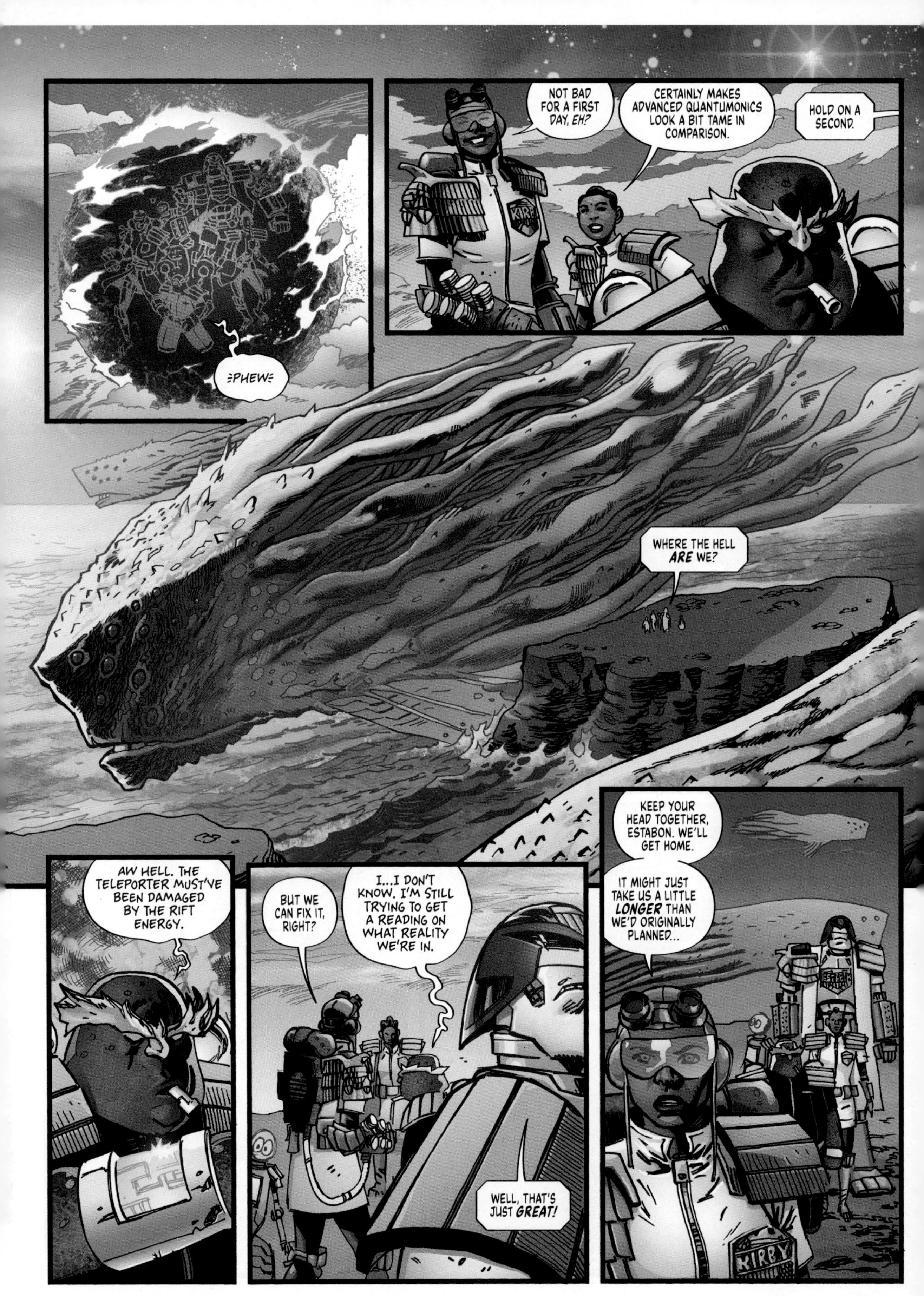

PHEW
NOT BAD FOR A FIRST DAY, *EH?*
CERTAINLY MAKES ADVANCED QUANTUMONICS LOOK A BIT TAME IN COMPARISON.
HOLD ON A SECOND.
WHERE THE HELL ***ARE*** WE?
AW HELL. THE TELEPORTER MUST'VE BEEN DAMAGED BY THE RIFT ENERGY.
BUT WE CAN FIX IT, RIGHT?
I...I DON'T KNOW. I'M STILL TRYING TO GET A READING ON WHAT REALITY WE'RE IN.
WELL, THAT'S JUST ***GREAT!***
KEEP YOUR HEAD TOGETHER, ESTABON. WE'LL GET HOME.
IT MIGHT JUST TAKE US A LITTLE ***LONGER*** THAN WE'D ORIGINALLY PLANNED...

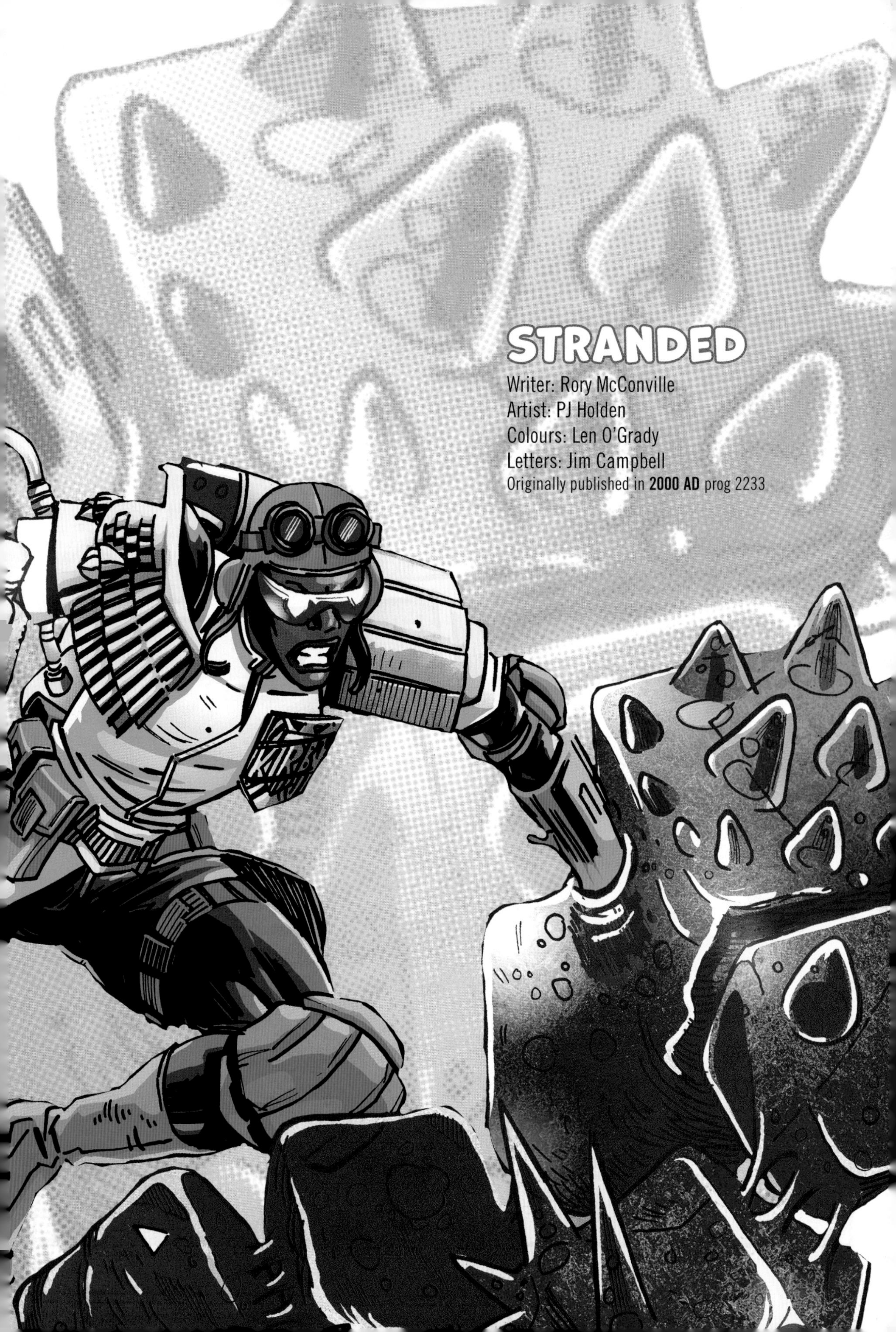

STRANDED

Writer: Rory McConville
Artist: PJ Holden
Colours: Len O'Grady
Letters: Jim Campbell
Originally published in **2000 AD** prog 2233

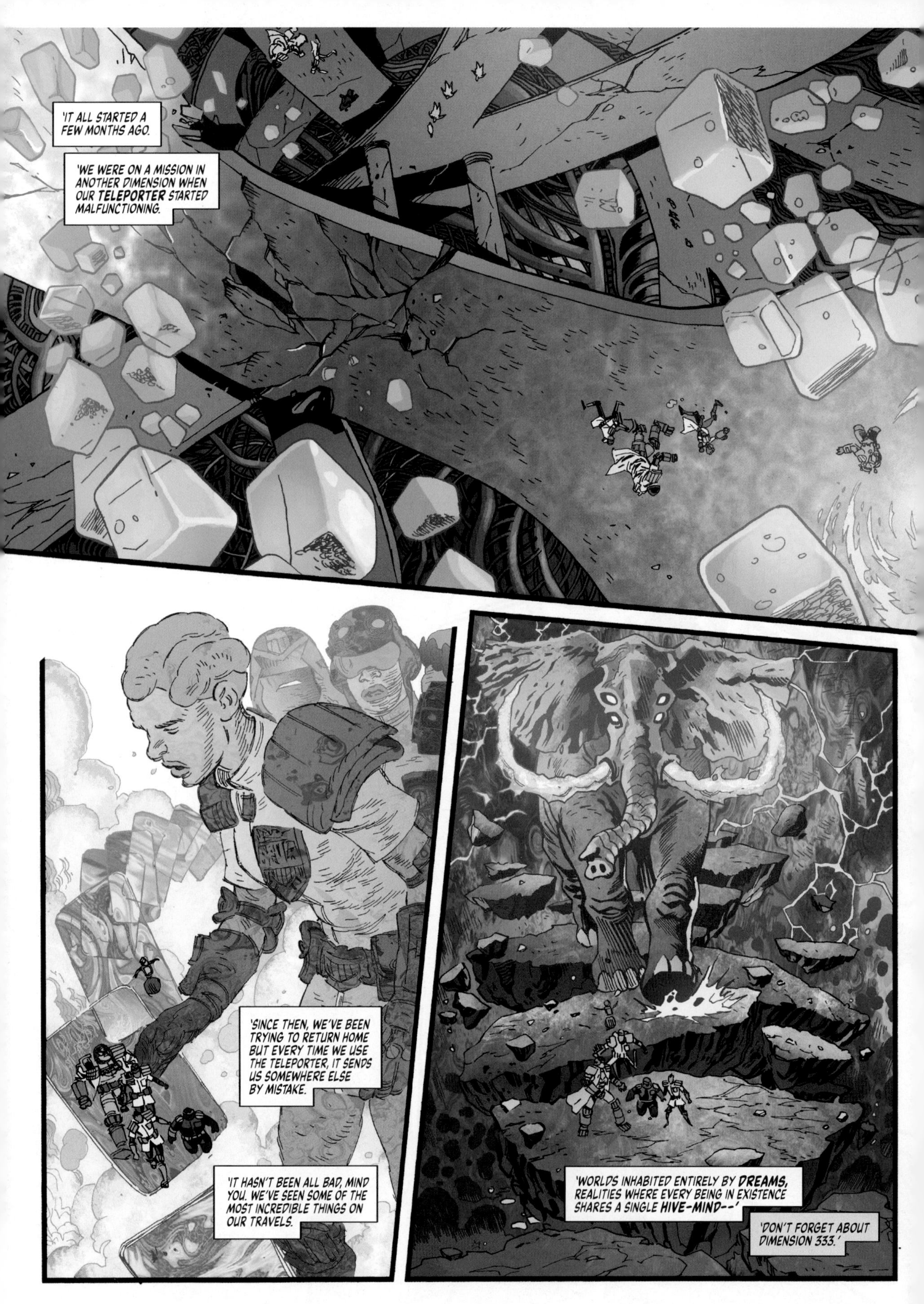
'IT ALL STARTED A FEW MONTHS AGO.
'WE WERE ON A MISSION IN ANOTHER DIMENSION WHEN OUR **TELEPORTER** STARTED MALFUNCTIONING.
'SINCE THEN, WE'VE BEEN TRYING TO RETURN HOME BUT EVERY TIME WE USE THE TELEPORTER, IT SENDS US SOMEWHERE ELSE BY MISTAKE.
'IT HASN'T BEEN ALL BAD, MIND YOU. WE'VE SEEN SOME OF THE MOST INCREDIBLE THINGS ON OUR TRAVELS.
'WORLDS INHABITED ENTIRELY BY **DREAMS,** REALITIES WHERE EVERY BEING IN EXISTENCE SHARES A SINGLE **HIVE-MIND--'**
'DON'T FORGET ABOUT DIMENSION 333.'

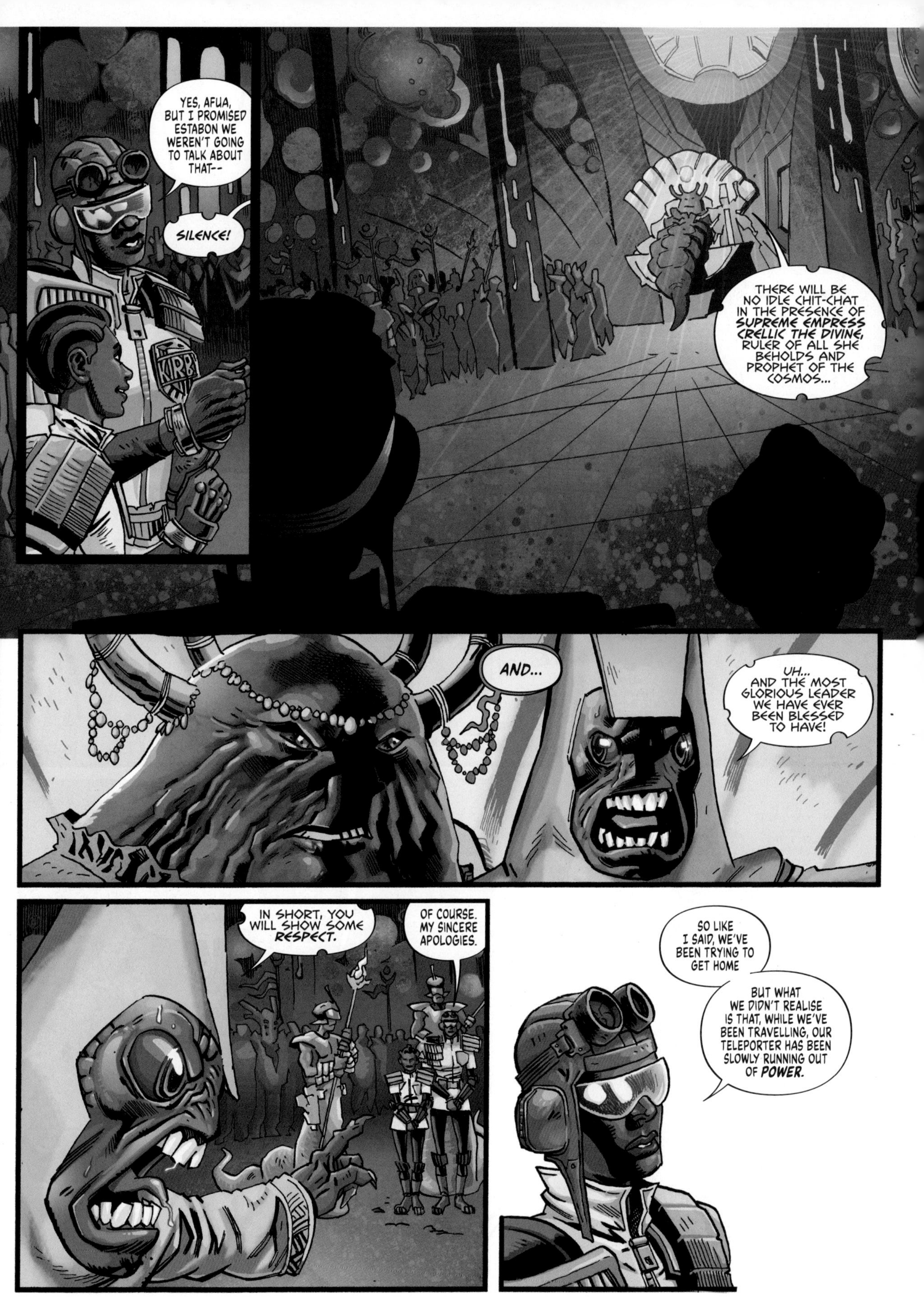
YES, AFUA, BUT I PROMISED ESTABON WE WEREN'T GOING TO TALK ABOUT THAT--
SILENCE!
THERE WILL BE NO IDLE CHIT-CHAT IN THE PRESENCE OF SUPREME EMPRESS CRELLIC THE DIVINE, RULER OF ALL SHE BEHOLDS AND PROPHET OF THE COSMOS...
AND...
UH... AND THE MOST GLORIOUS LEADER WE HAVE EVER BEEN BLESSED TO HAVE!
IN SHORT, YOU WILL SHOW SOME RESPECT.
OF COURSE. MY SINCERE APOLOGIES.
SO LIKE I SAID, WE'VE BEEN TRYING TO GET HOME
BUT WHAT WE DIDN'T REALISE IS THAT, WHILE WE'VE BEEN TRAVELLING, OUR TELEPORTER HAS BEEN SLOWLY RUNNING OUT OF POWER.

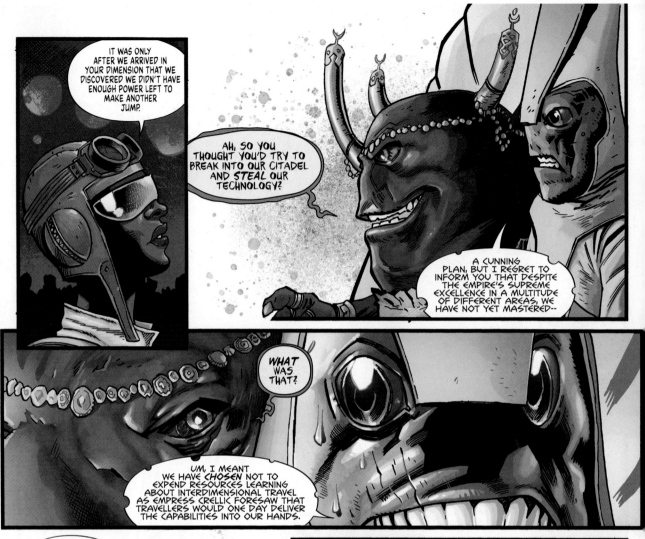

IT WAS ONLY AFTER WE ARRIVED IN YOUR DIMENSION THAT WE DISCOVERED WE DIDN'T HAVE ENOUGH POWER LEFT TO MAKE ANOTHER JUMP.

AH, SO YOU THOUGHT YOU'D TRY TO BREAK INTO OUR CITADEL AND *STEAL* OUR TECHNOLOGY?

A CUNNING PLAN, BUT I REGRET TO INFORM YOU THAT DESPITE THE EMPIRE'S SUPREME EXCELLENCE IN A MULTITUDE OF DIFFERENT AREAS, WE HAVE NOT YET MASTERED--

WHAT WAS THAT?

UM, I MEANT WE HAVE *CHOSEN* NOT TO EXPEND RESOURCES LEARNING ABOUT INTERDIMENSIONAL TRAVEL AS EMPRESS CRELLIC FORESAW THAT TRAVELLERS WOULD ONE DAY DELIVER THE CAPABILITIES INTO OUR HANDS.

OUR SCIENTISTS LOOK FORWARD TO LEARNING ALL ABOUT *THIS* MYSTERIOUS DEVICE.

I'M AFRAID *YOU* WILL BE SPENDING THE REST OF YOUR EXISTENCE IN OUR DUNGEONS, HOWEVER.

OH, YOU THINK...?

SORRY, THERE'S BEEN A MISTAKE. MY GAUNTLET, GREAT AND ALL AS IT IS, ISN'T CAPABLE OF INTERDIMENSIONAL TRAVEL.

THE TELE-PORTER BELONGS TO OUR COLLEAGUE, *BLACKCURRANT.*

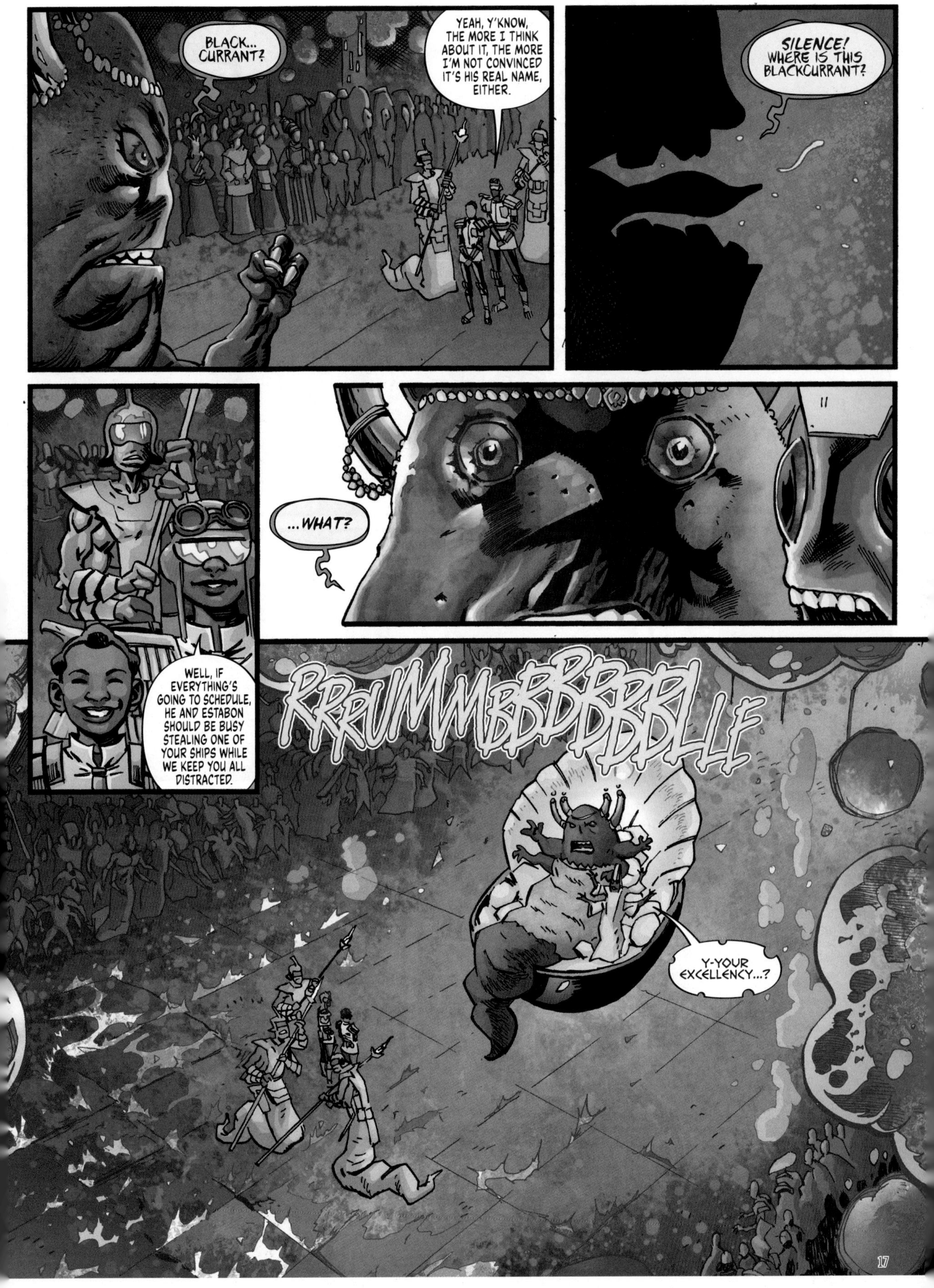
BLACK... CURRANT?
YEAH, Y'KNOW, THE MORE I THINK ABOUT IT, THE MORE I'M NOT CONVINCED IT'S HIS REAL NAME, EITHER.
SILENCE! WHERE IS THIS BLACKCURRANT?
WELL, IF EVERYTHING'S GOING TO SCHEDULE, HE AND ESTABON SHOULD BE BUSY STEALING ONE OF YOUR SHIPS WHILE WE KEEP YOU ALL DISTRACTED.
...WHAT?
RRRUMMBBBBBBBLLE
Y-YOUR EXCELLENCY...?

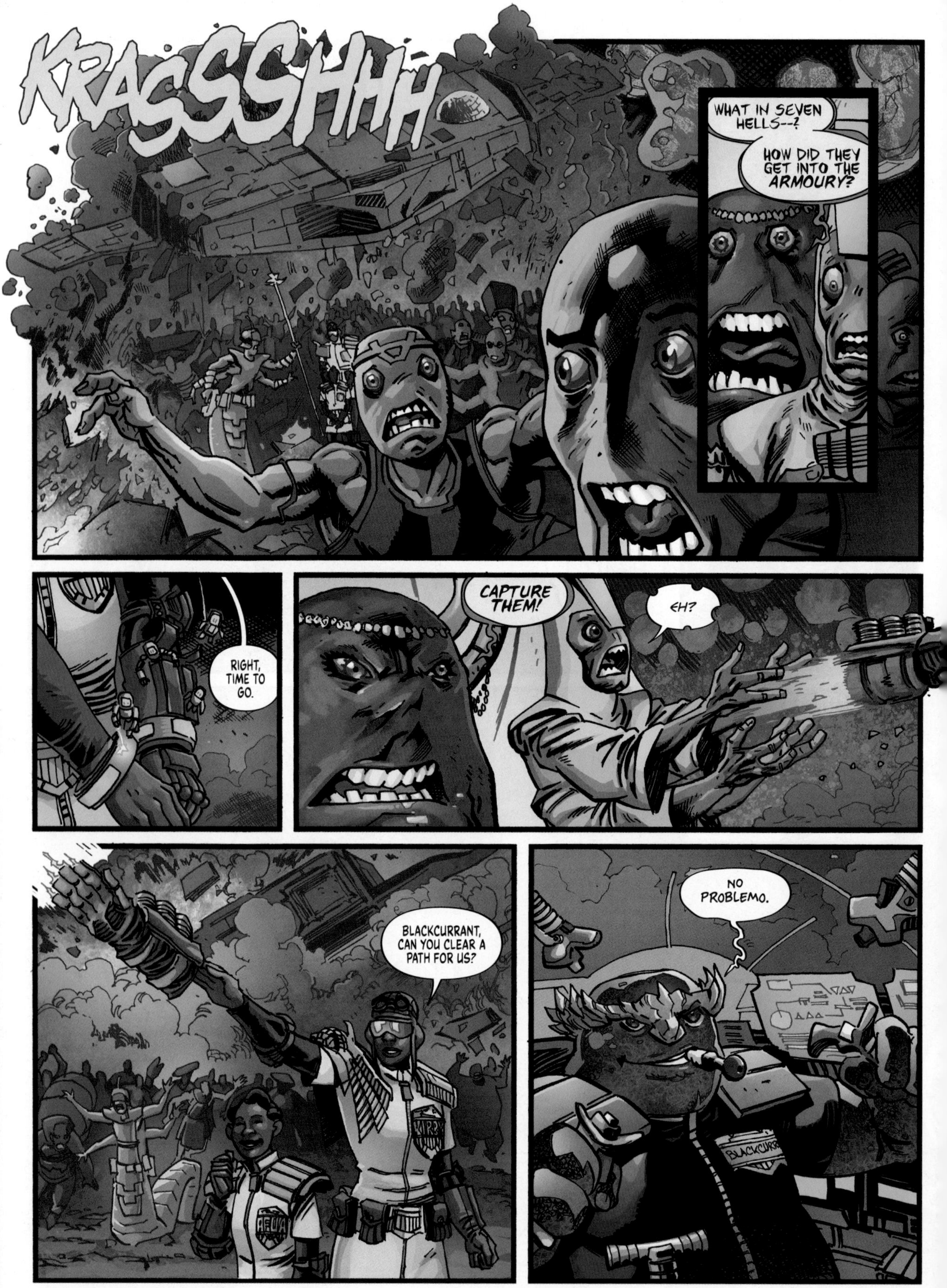
KRASSSHHH
WHAT IN SEVEN HELLS--?
HOW DID THEY GET INTO THE ARMOURY?
RIGHT, TIME TO GO.
CAPTURE THEM!
EH?
BLACKCURRANT, CAN YOU CLEAR A PATH FOR US?
NO PROBLEMO.

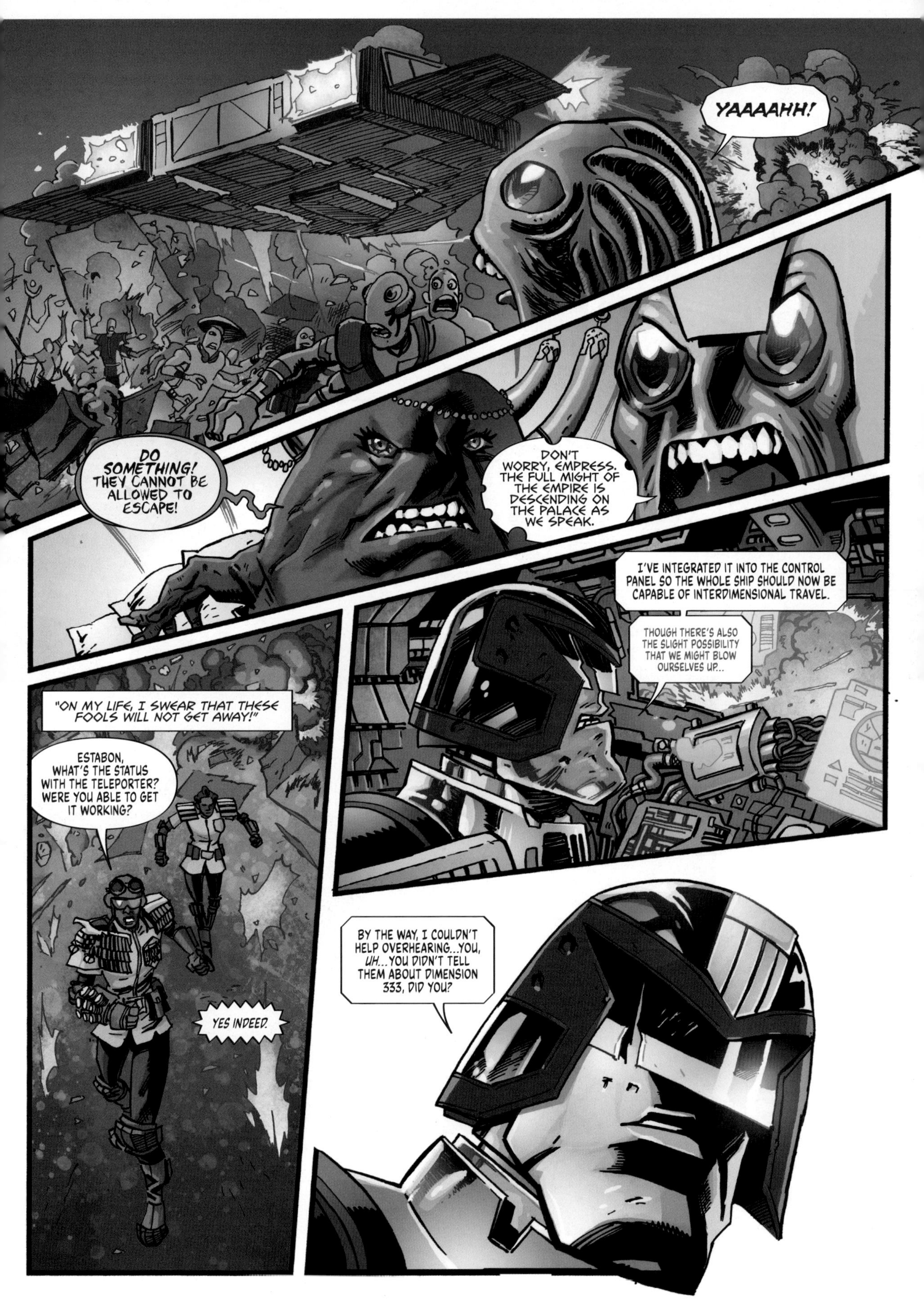
YAAAAHH!
DO SOMETHING! THEY CANNOT BE ALLOWED TO ESCAPE!
DON'T WORRY, EMPRESS. THE FULL MIGHT OF THE EMPIRE IS DESCENDING ON THE PALACE AS WE SPEAK.
"ON MY LIFE, I SWEAR THAT THESE FOOLS WILL NOT GET AWAY!"
ESTABON, WHAT'S THE STATUS WITH THE TELEPORTER? WERE YOU ABLE TO GET IT WORKING?
YES INDEED.
I'VE INTEGRATED IT INTO THE CONTROL PANEL SO THE WHOLE SHIP SHOULD NOW BE CAPABLE OF INTERDIMENSIONAL TRAVEL.
THOUGH THERE'S ALSO THE SLIGHT POSSIBILITY THAT WE MIGHT BLOW OURSELVES UP...
BY THE WAY, I COULDN'T HELP OVERHEARING...YOU, UH...YOU DIDN'T TELL THEM ABOUT DIMENSION 333, DID YOU?

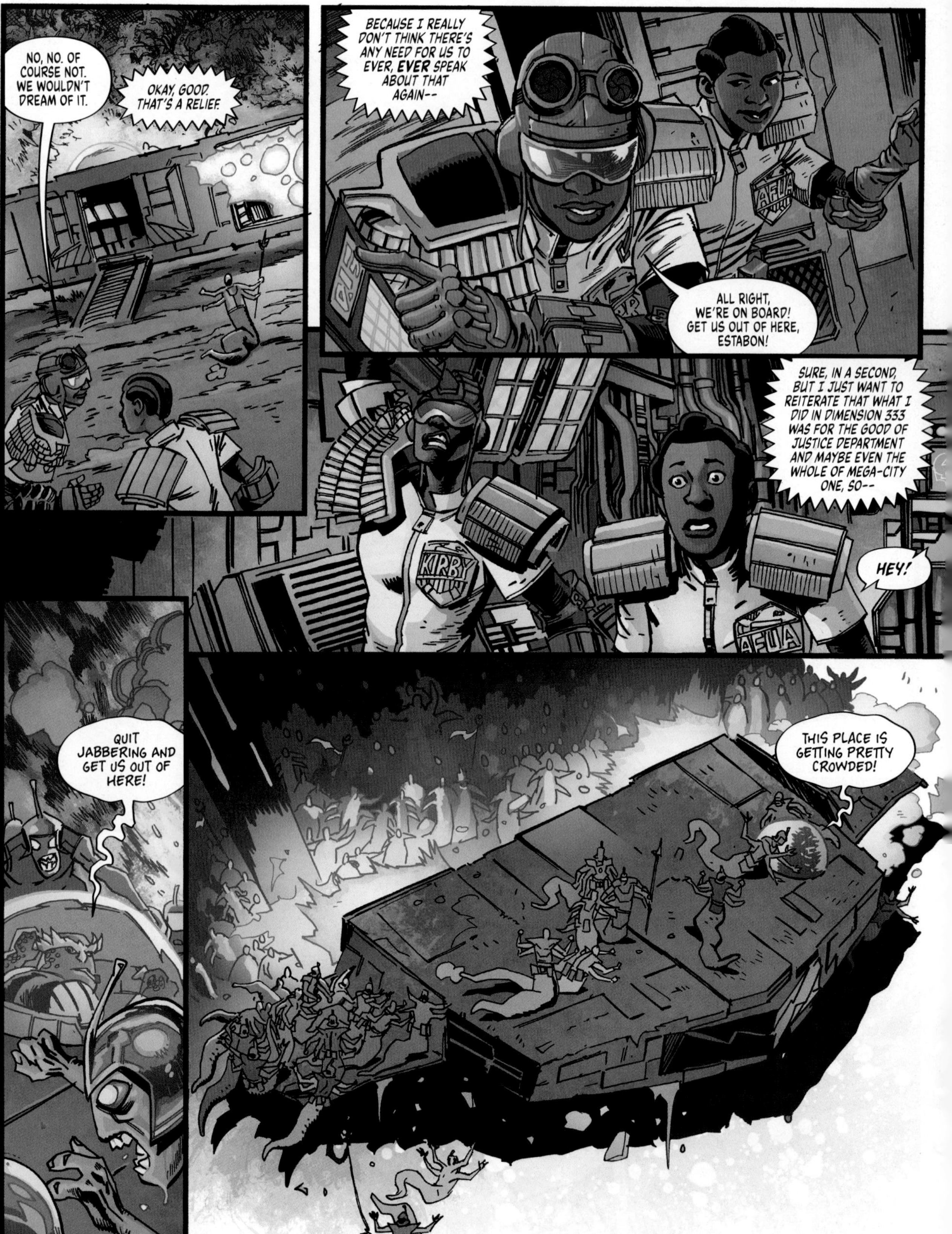
NO, NO. OF COURSE NOT. WE WOULDN'T DREAM OF IT.
OKAY, GOOD. THAT'S A RELIEF.
BECAUSE I REALLY DON'T THINK THERE'S ANY NEED FOR US TO EVER, **EVER** SPEAK ABOUT THAT AGAIN--
ALL RIGHT, WE'RE ON BOARD! GET US OUT OF HERE, ESTABON!
SURE, IN A SECOND, BUT I JUST WANT TO REITERATE THAT WHAT I DID IN DIMENSION 333 WAS FOR THE GOOD OF JUSTICE DEPARTMENT AND MAYBE EVEN THE WHOLE OF MEGA-CITY ONE, SO--
HEY!
KIRBY
AFUA
QUIT JABBERING AND GET US OUT OF HERE!
THIS PLACE IS GETTING PRETTY CROWDED!

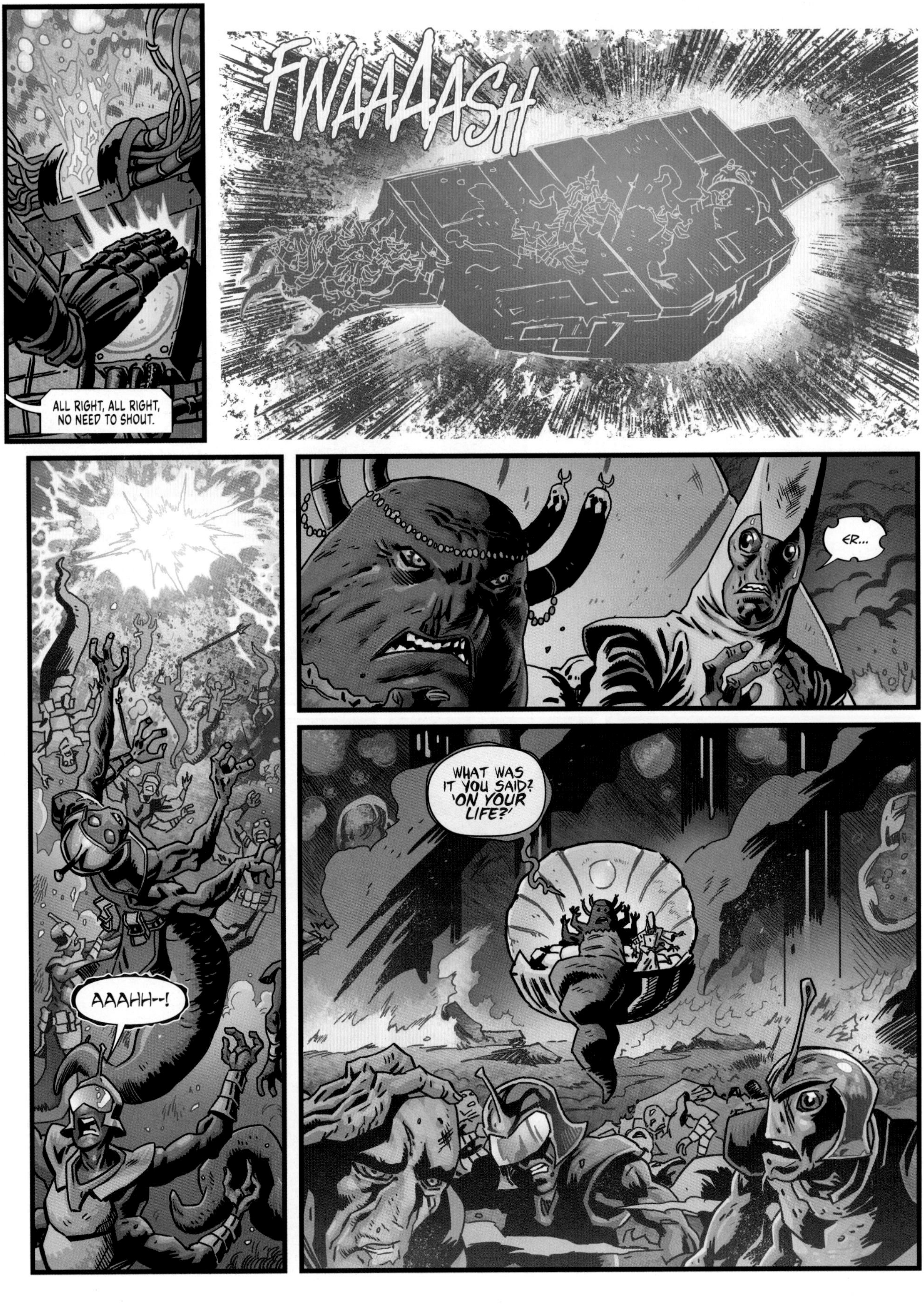
ALL RIGHT, ALL RIGHT, NO NEED TO SHOUT.
FWAAAASH
AAAHH--!
ER...
WHAT WAS IT YOU SAID? 'ON YOUR LIFE?'

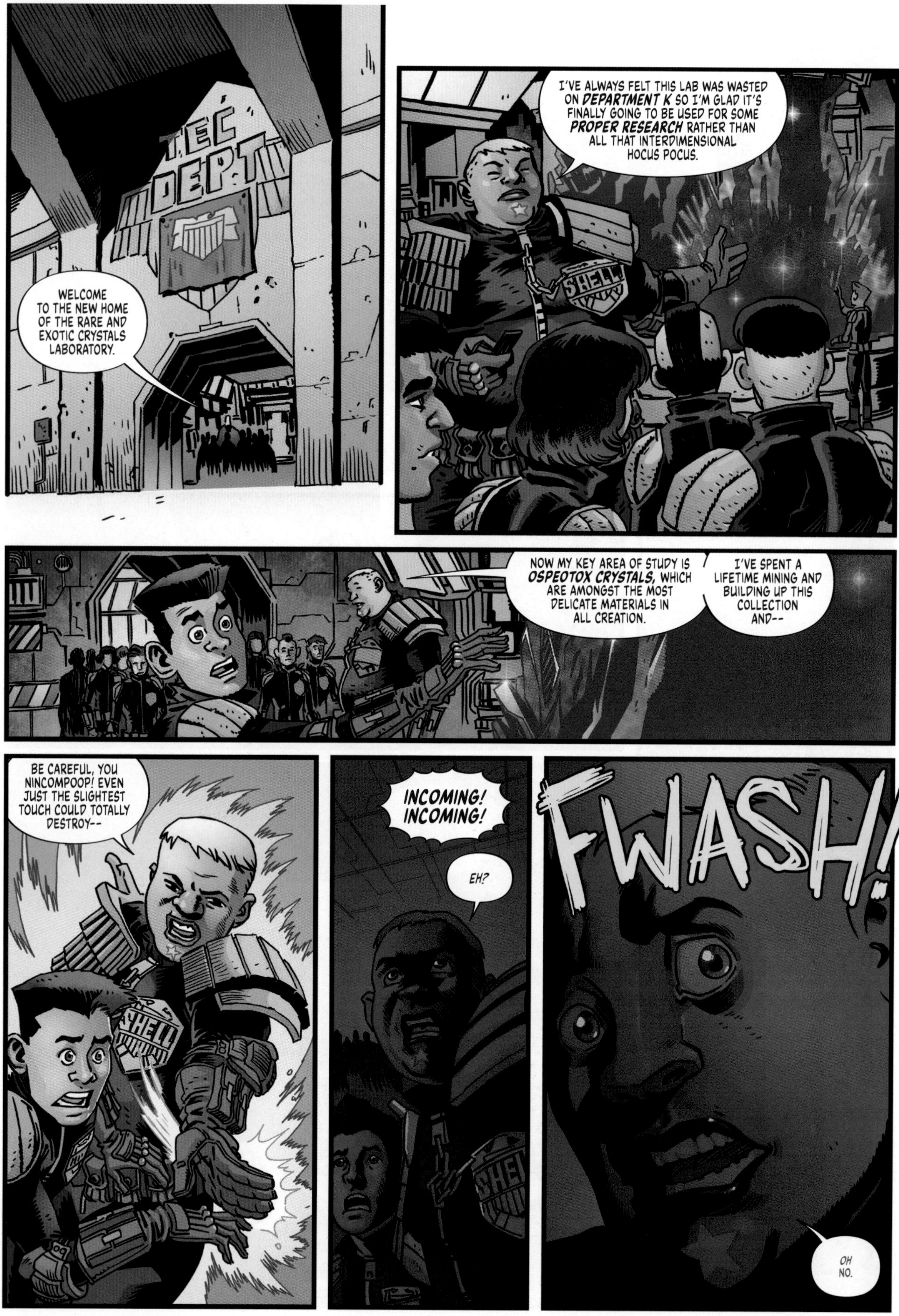
TEC DEPT
WELCOME TO THE NEW HOME OF THE RARE AND EXOTIC CRYSTALS LABORATORY.
I'VE ALWAYS FELT THIS LAB WAS WASTED ON DEPARTMENT K SO I'M GLAD IT'S FINALLY GOING TO BE USED FOR SOME PROPER RESEARCH RATHER THAN ALL THAT INTERDIMENSIONAL HOCUS POCUS.
SHELL
NOW MY KEY AREA OF STUDY IS OSPEOTOX CRYSTALS, WHICH ARE AMONGST THE MOST DELICATE MATERIALS IN ALL CREATION.
I'VE SPENT A LIFETIME MINING AND BUILDING UP THIS COLLECTION AND--
BE CAREFUL, YOU NINCOMPOOP! EVEN JUST THE SLIGHTEST TOUCH COULD TOTALLY DESTROY--
SHELL
INCOMING! INCOMING!
EH?
FWASH!
OH NO.

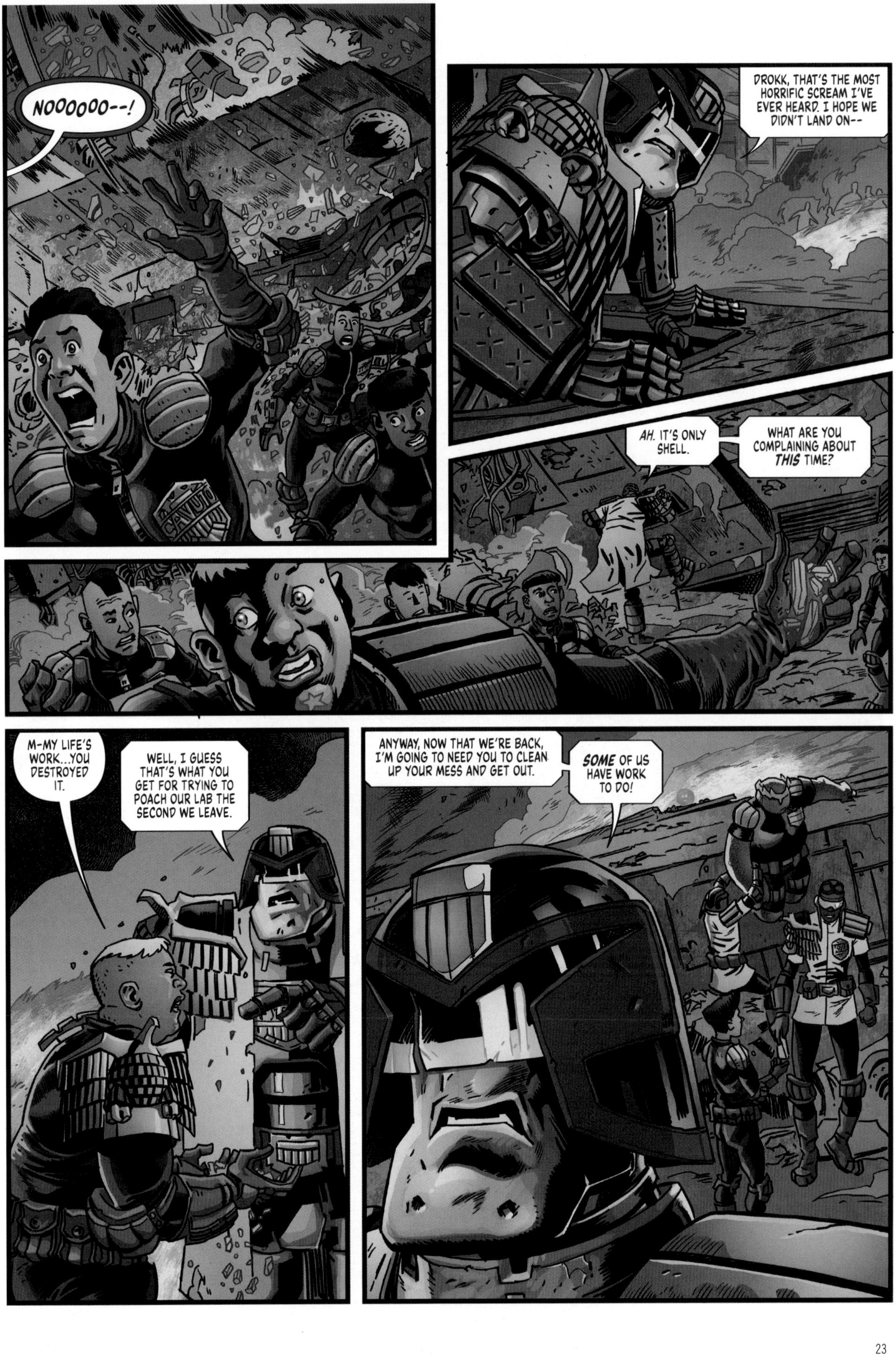
NOOOOOO--!
DROKK, THAT'S THE MOST HORRIFIC SCREAM I'VE EVER HEARD. I HOPE WE DIDN'T LAND ON--
AH. IT'S ONLY SHELL.
WHAT ARE YOU COMPLAINING ABOUT THIS TIME?
M-MY LIFE'S WORK...YOU DESTROYED IT.
WELL, I GUESS THAT'S WHAT YOU GET FOR TRYING TO POACH OUR LAB THE SECOND WE LEAVE.
ANYWAY, NOW THAT WE'RE BACK, I'M GOING TO NEED YOU TO CLEAN UP YOUR MESS AND GET OUT.
SOME OF US HAVE WORK TO DO!

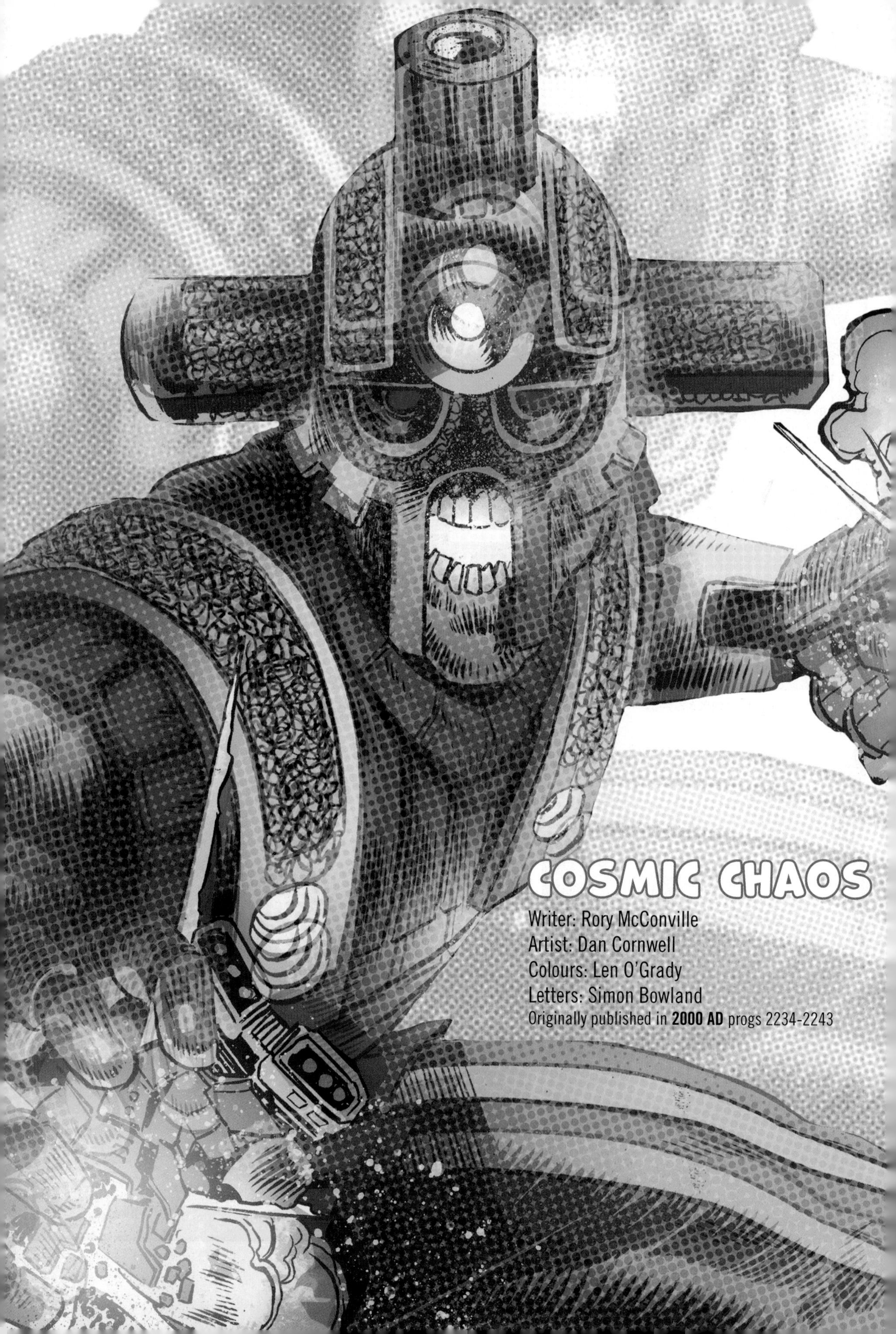

COSMIC CHAOS

Writer: Rory McConville
Artist: Dan Cornwell
Colours: Len O'Grady
Letters: Simon Bowland

Originally published in **2000 AD** progs 2234-2243

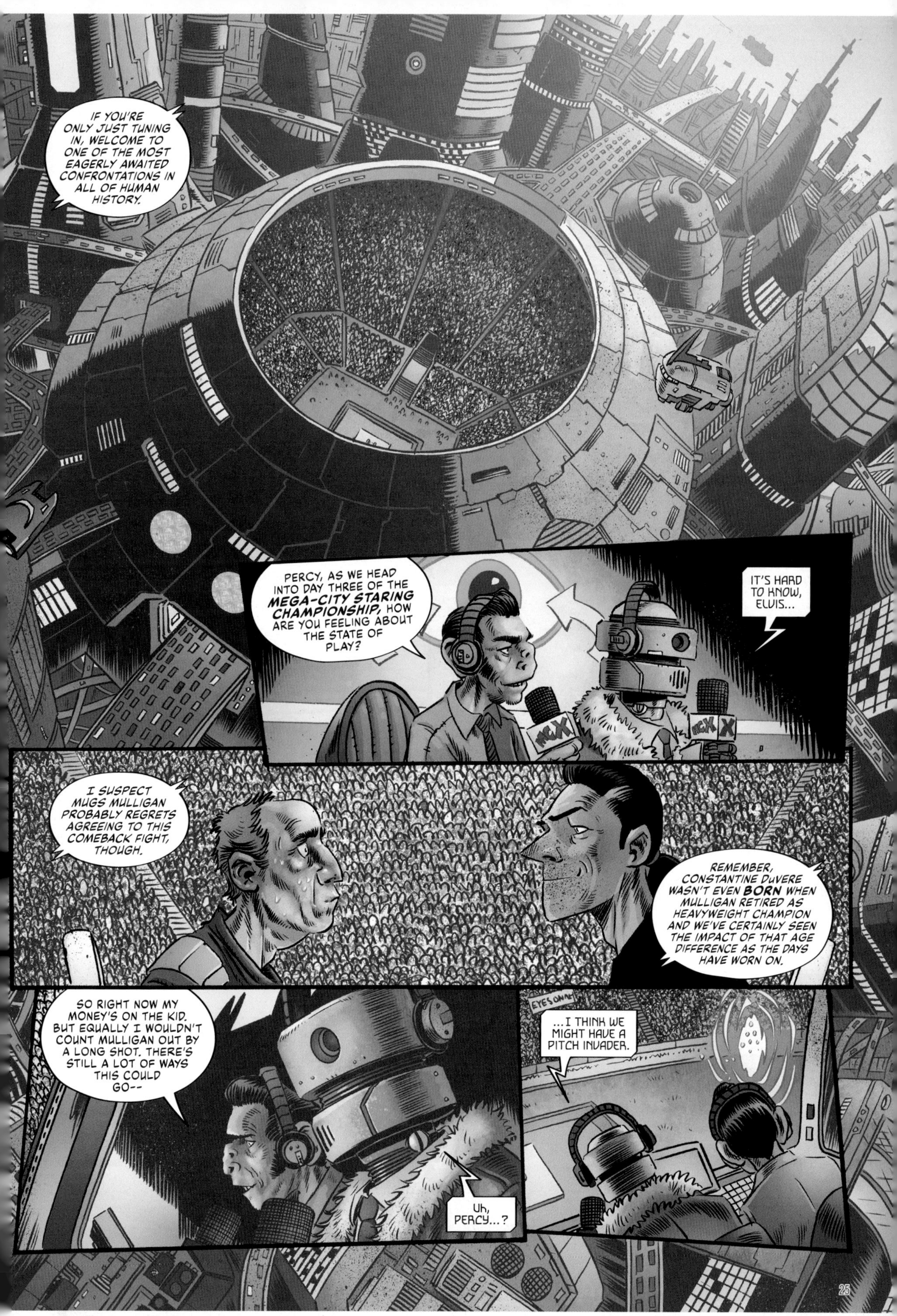
IF YOU'RE ONLY JUST TUNING IN, WELCOME TO ONE OF THE MOST EAGERLY AWAITED CONFRONTATIONS IN ALL OF HUMAN HISTORY.
PERCY, AS WE HEAD INTO DAY THREE OF THE MEGA-CITY STARING CHAMPIONSHIP, HOW ARE YOU FEELING ABOUT THE STATE OF PLAY?
IT'S HARD TO KNOW, ELVIS...
I SUSPECT MUGS MULLIGAN PROBABLY REGRETS AGREEING TO THIS COMEBACK FIGHT, THOUGH.
REMEMBER, CONSTANTINE DuVERE WASN'T EVEN BORN WHEN MULLIGAN RETIRED AS HEAVYWEIGHT CHAMPION AND WE'VE CERTAINLY SEEN THE IMPACT OF THAT AGE DIFFERENCE AS THE DAYS HAVE WORN ON.
SO RIGHT NOW MY MONEY'S ON THE KID. BUT EQUALLY I WOULDN'T COUNT MULLIGAN OUT BY A LONG SHOT. THERE'S STILL A LOT OF WAYS THIS COULD GO--
Uh, PERCY...?
...I THINK WE MIGHT HAVE A PITCH INVADER.

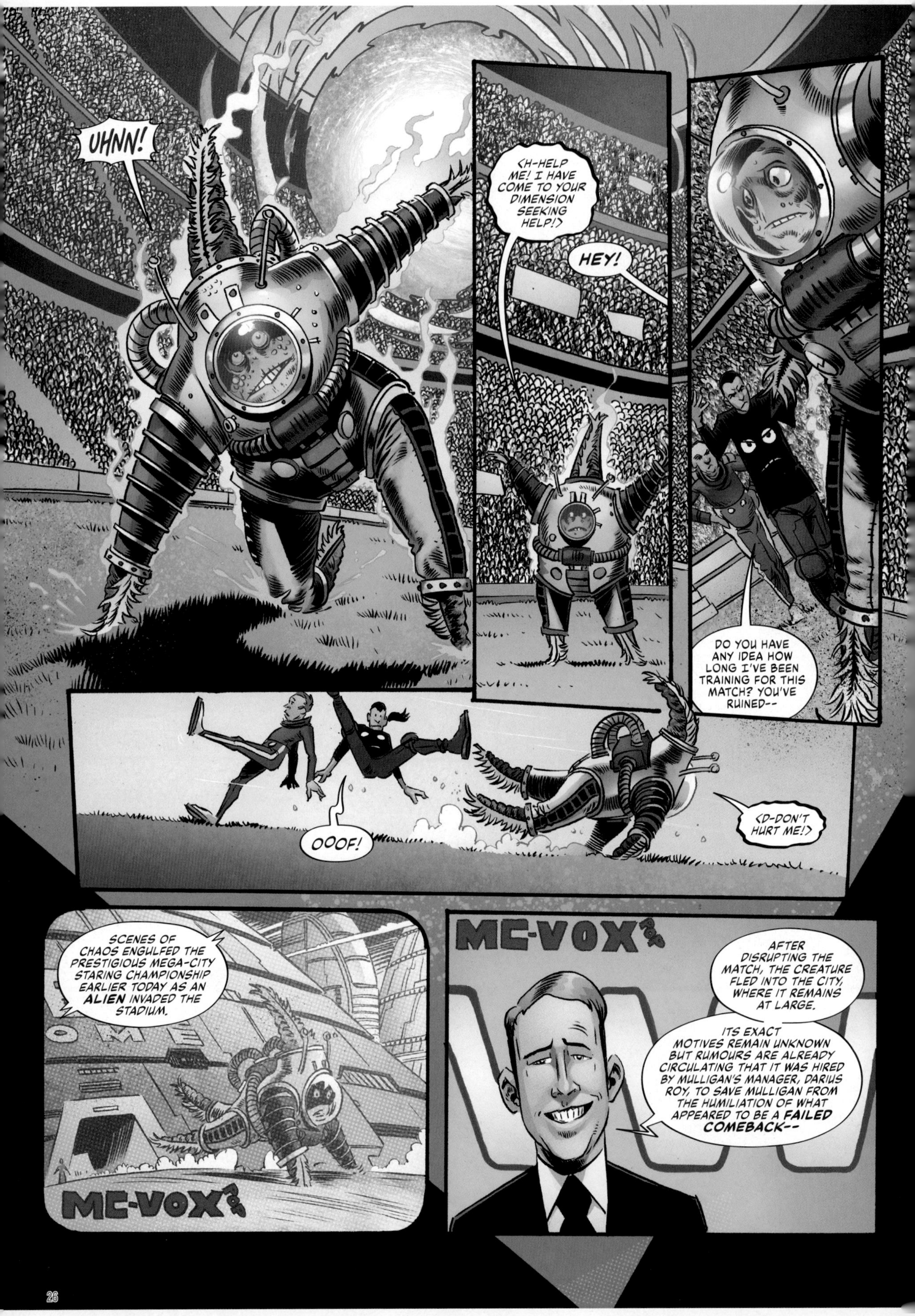
UHNN!
<H-HELP ME! I HAVE COME TO YOUR DIMENSION SEEKING HELP!>
HEY!
DO YOU HAVE ANY IDEA HOW LONG I'VE BEEN TRAINING FOR THIS MATCH? YOU'VE RUINED--
OOOF!
<D-DON'T HURT ME!>
SCENES OF CHAOS ENGULFED THE PRESTIGIOUS MEGA-CITY STARING CHAMPIONSHIP EARLIER TODAY AS AN ALIEN INVADED THE STADIUM.
MC-VOX POP
MC-VOX POP
AFTER DISRUPTING THE MATCH, THE CREATURE FLED INTO THE CITY, WHERE IT REMAINS AT LARGE.
ITS EXACT MOTIVES REMAIN UNKNOWN BUT RUMOURS ARE ALREADY CIRCULATING THAT IT WAS HIRED BY MULLIGAN'S MANAGER, DARIUS ROY, TO SAVE MULLIGAN FROM THE HUMILIATION OF WHAT APPEARED TO BE A FAILED COMEBACK--

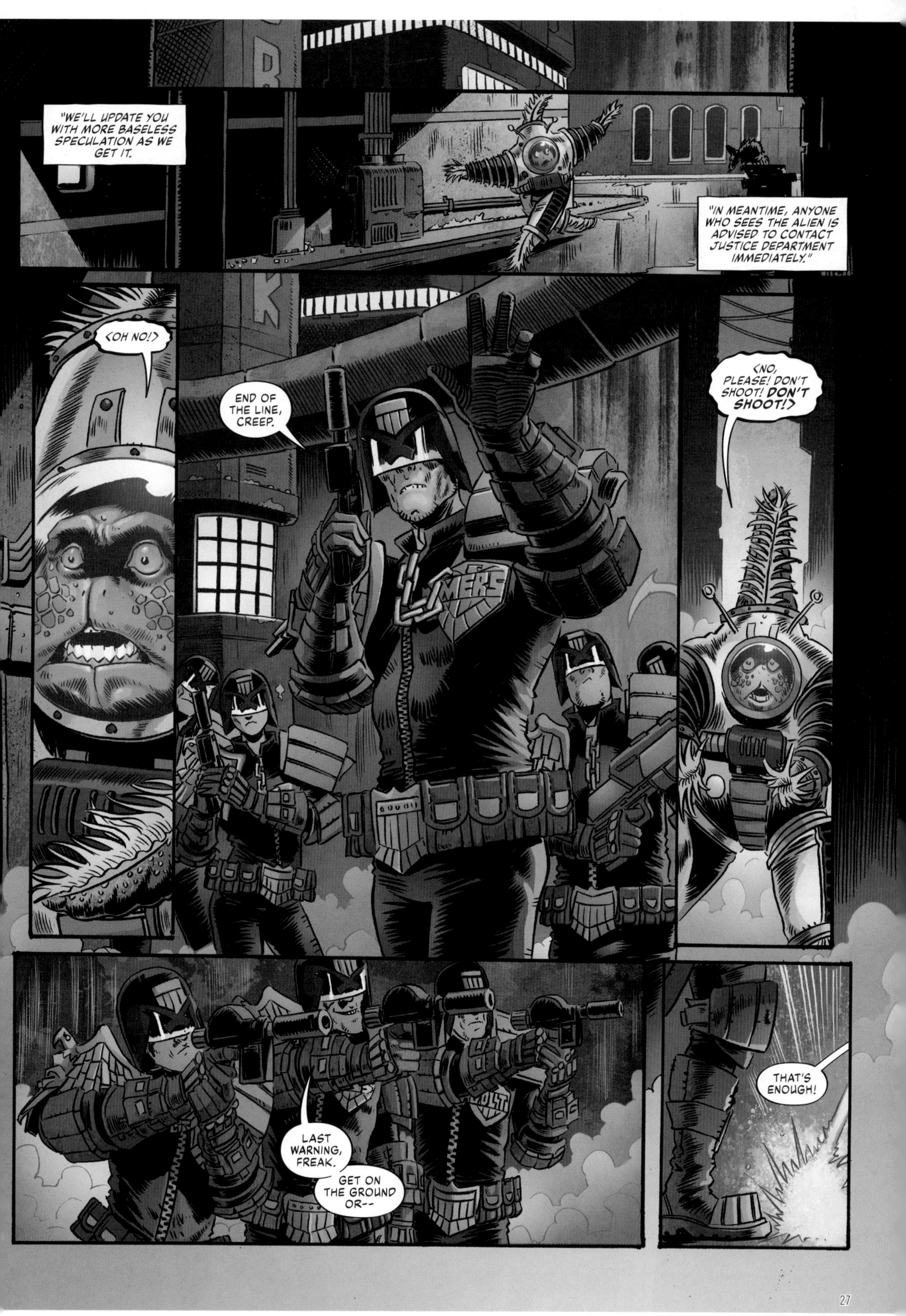

"WE'LL UPDATE YOU WITH MORE BASELESS SPECULATION AS WE GET IT.
"IN MEANTIME, ANYONE WHO SEES THE ALIEN IS ADVISED TO CONTACT JUSTICE DEPARTMENT IMMEDIATELY."
<OH NO!>
END OF THE LINE, CREEP.
<NO, PLEASE! DON'T SHOOT! **DON'T SHOOT!**>
LAST WARNING, FREAK.
GET ON THE GROUND OR--
THAT'S ENOUGH!

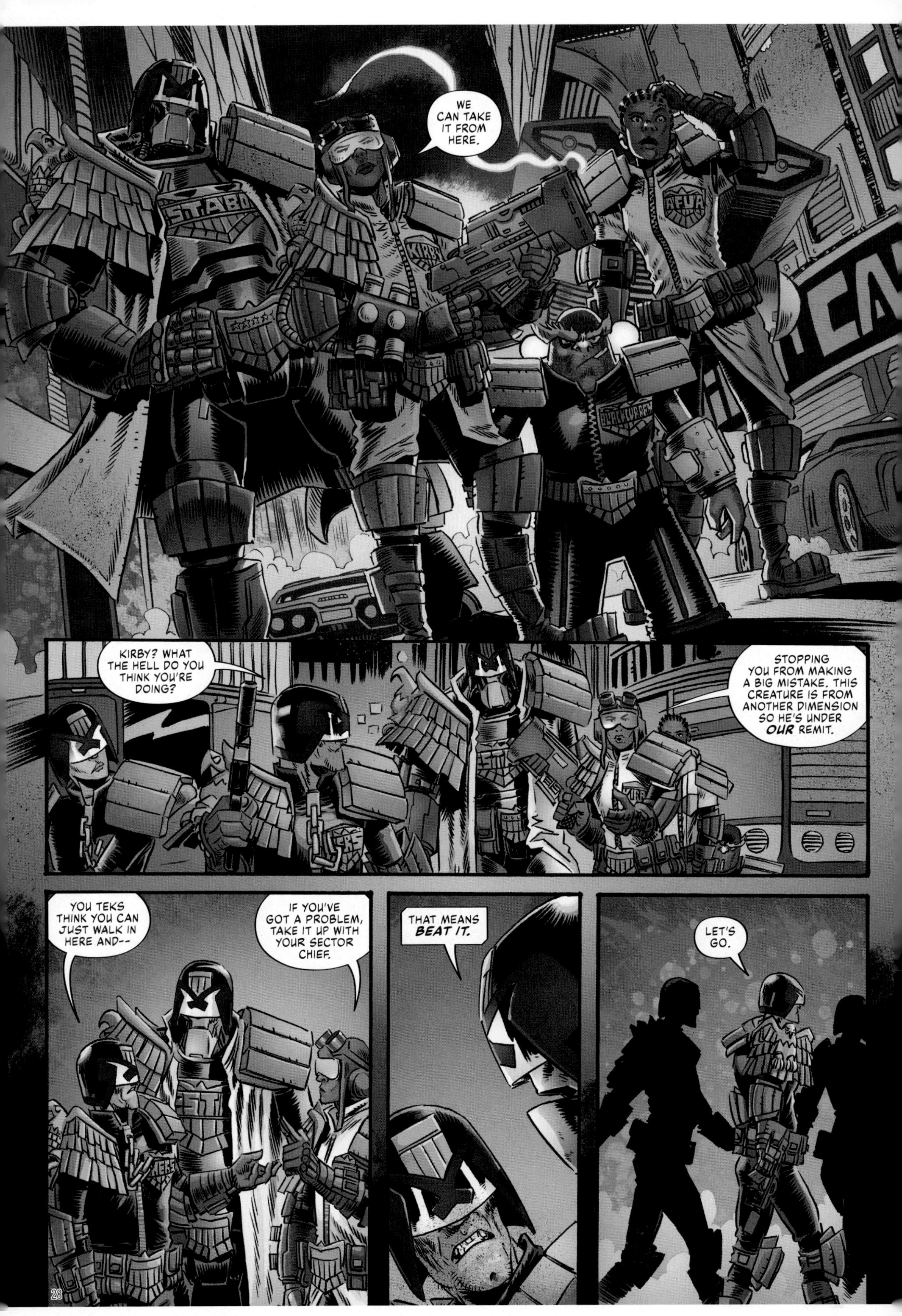
WE CAN TAKE IT FROM HERE.
STABO
KIRBY
AFUA
KIRBY? WHAT THE HELL DO YOU THINK YOU'RE DOING?
STOPPING YOU FROM MAKING A BIG MISTAKE. THIS CREATURE IS FROM ANOTHER DIMENSION SO HE'S UNDER OUR REMIT.
YOU TEKS THINK YOU CAN JUST WALK IN HERE AND--
IF YOU'VE GOT A PROBLEM, TAKE IT UP WITH YOUR SECTOR CHIEF.
THAT MEANS BEAT IT.
LET'S GO.

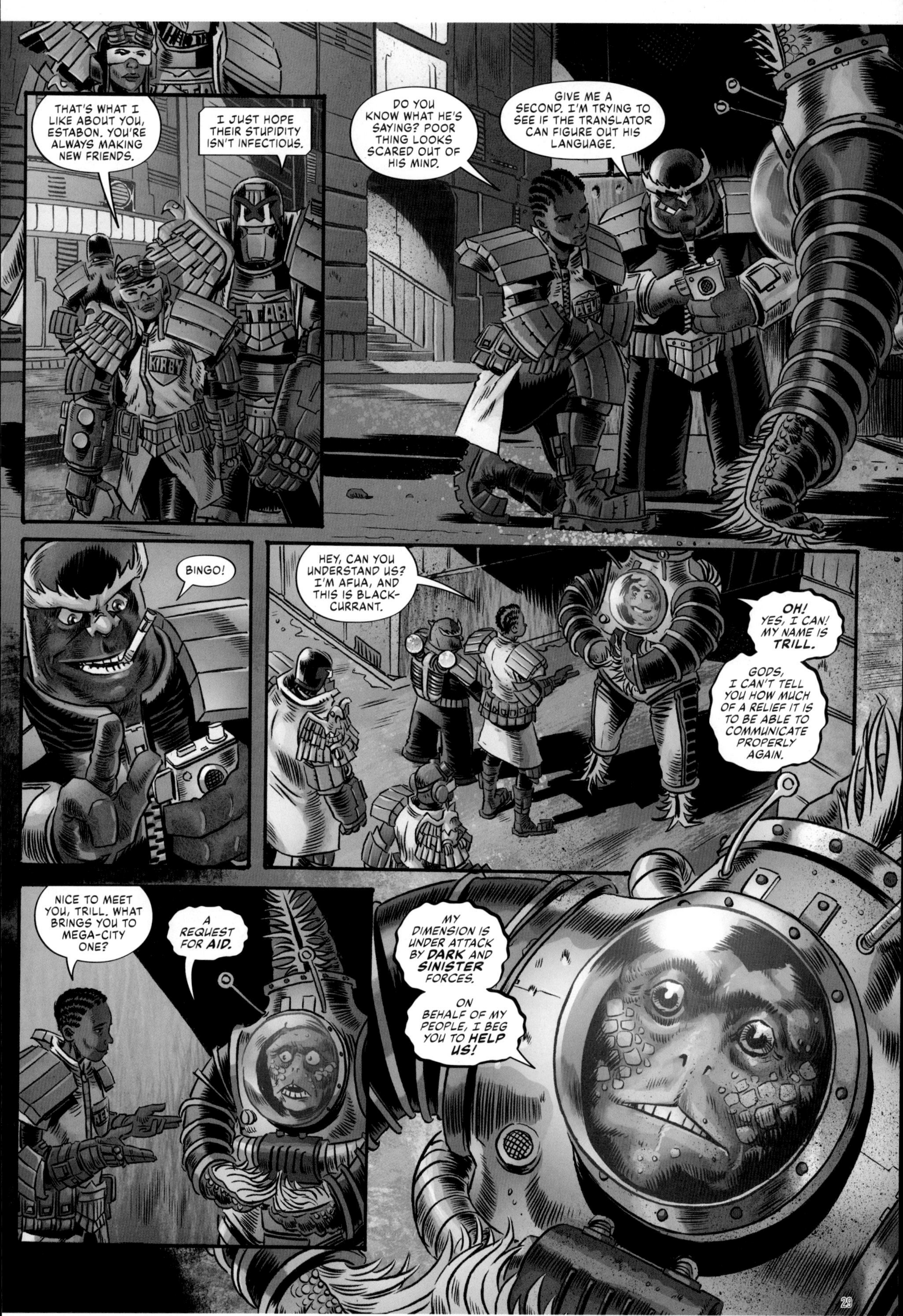
THAT'S WHAT I LIKE ABOUT YOU, ESTABON. YOU'RE ALWAYS MAKING NEW FRIENDS.
I JUST HOPE THEIR STUPIDITY ISN'T INFECTIOUS.
DO YOU KNOW WHAT HE'S SAYING? POOR THING LOOKS SCARED OUT OF HIS MIND.
GIVE ME A SECOND. I'M TRYING TO SEE IF THE TRANSLATOR CAN FIGURE OUT HIS LANGUAGE.
KIRBY
ESTABO
AFUA
BINGO!
HEY, CAN YOU UNDERSTAND US? I'M AFUA, AND THIS IS BLACK-CURRANT.
OH! YES, I CAN! MY NAME IS TRILL.
GODS, I CAN'T TELL YOU HOW MUCH OF A RELIEF IT IS TO BE ABLE TO COMMUNICATE PROPERLY AGAIN.
NICE TO MEET YOU, TRILL. WHAT BRINGS YOU TO MEGA-CITY ONE?
A REQUEST FOR AID.
MY DIMENSION IS UNDER ATTACK BY DARK AND SINISTER FORCES.
ON BEHALF OF MY PEOPLE, I BEG YOU TO HELP US!

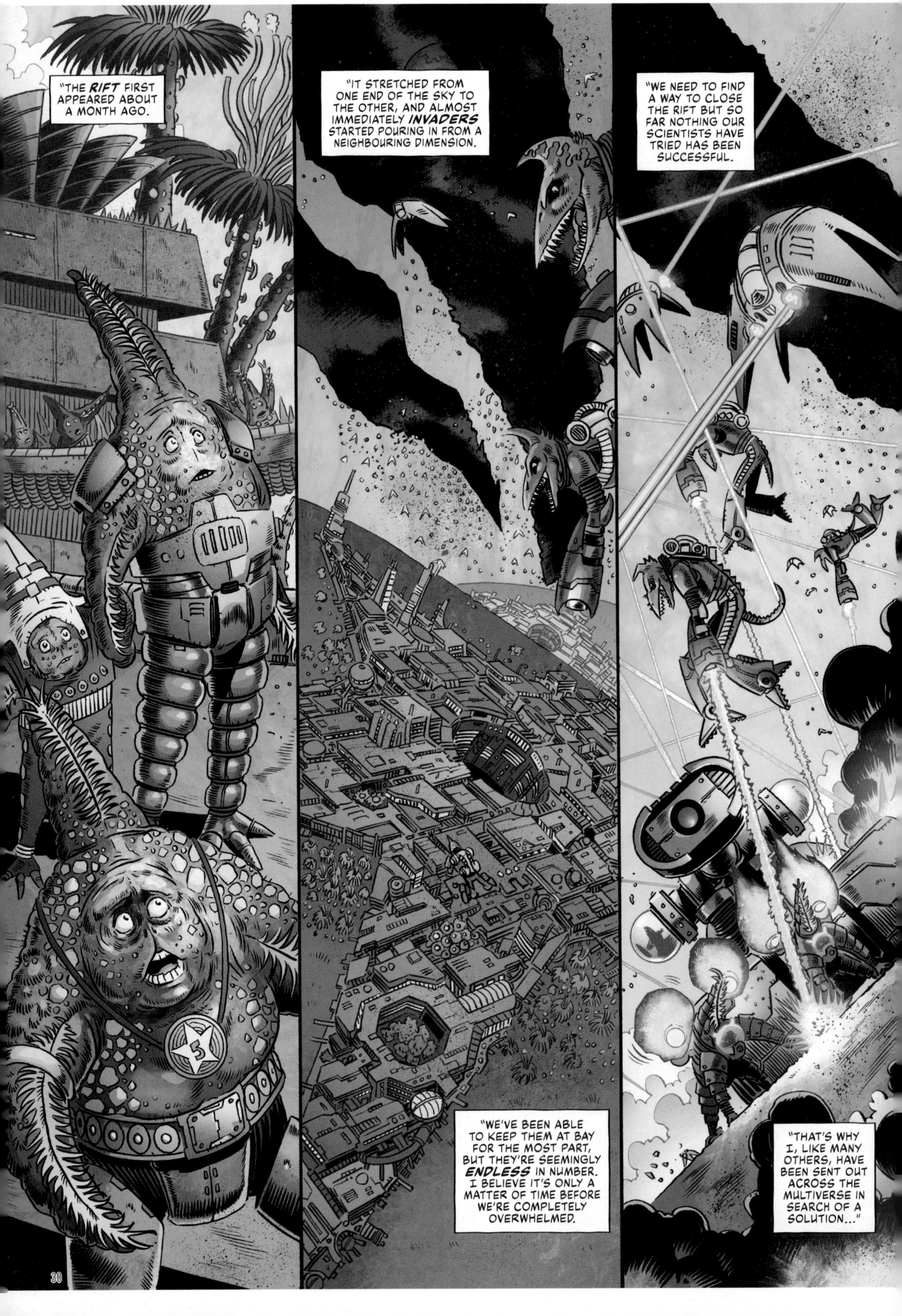
"THE RIFT FIRST APPEARED ABOUT A MONTH AGO.
"IT STRETCHED FROM ONE END OF THE SKY TO THE OTHER, AND ALMOST IMMEDIATELY INVADERS STARTED POURING IN FROM A NEIGHBOURING DIMENSION.
"WE'VE BEEN ABLE TO KEEP THEM AT BAY FOR THE MOST PART, BUT THEY'RE SEEMINGLY ENDLESS IN NUMBER. I BELIEVE IT'S ONLY A MATTER OF TIME BEFORE WE'RE COMPLETELY OVERWHELMED.
"WE NEED TO FIND A WAY TO CLOSE THE RIFT BUT SO FAR NOTHING OUR SCIENTISTS HAVE TRIED HAS BEEN SUCCESSFUL.
"THAT'S WHY I, LIKE MANY OTHERS, HAVE BEEN SENT OUT ACROSS THE MULTIVERSE IN SEARCH OF A SOLUTION..."

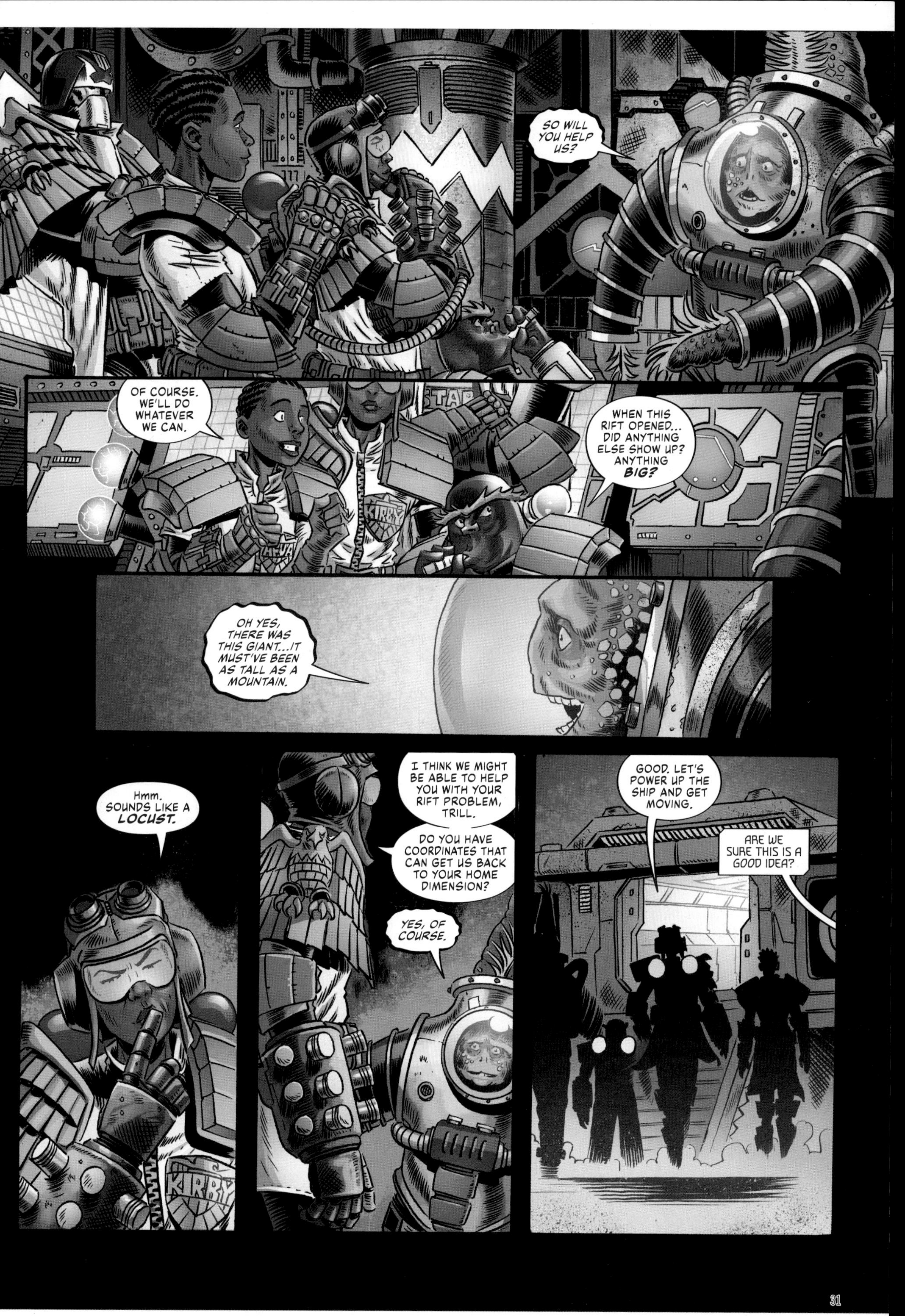
SO WILL YOU HELP US?
OF COURSE. WE'LL DO WHATEVER WE CAN.
WHEN THIS RIFT OPENED... DID ANYTHING ELSE SHOW UP? ANYTHING BIG?
OH YES, THERE WAS THIS GIANT...IT MUST'VE BEEN AS TALL AS A MOUNTAIN.
Hmm. SOUNDS LIKE A LOCUST.
I THINK WE MIGHT BE ABLE TO HELP YOU WITH YOUR RIFT PROBLEM, TRILL.
DO YOU HAVE COORDINATES THAT CAN GET US BACK TO YOUR HOME DIMENSION?
YES, OF COURSE.
GOOD. LET'S POWER UP THE SHIP AND GET MOVING.
ARE WE SURE THIS IS A GOOD IDEA?

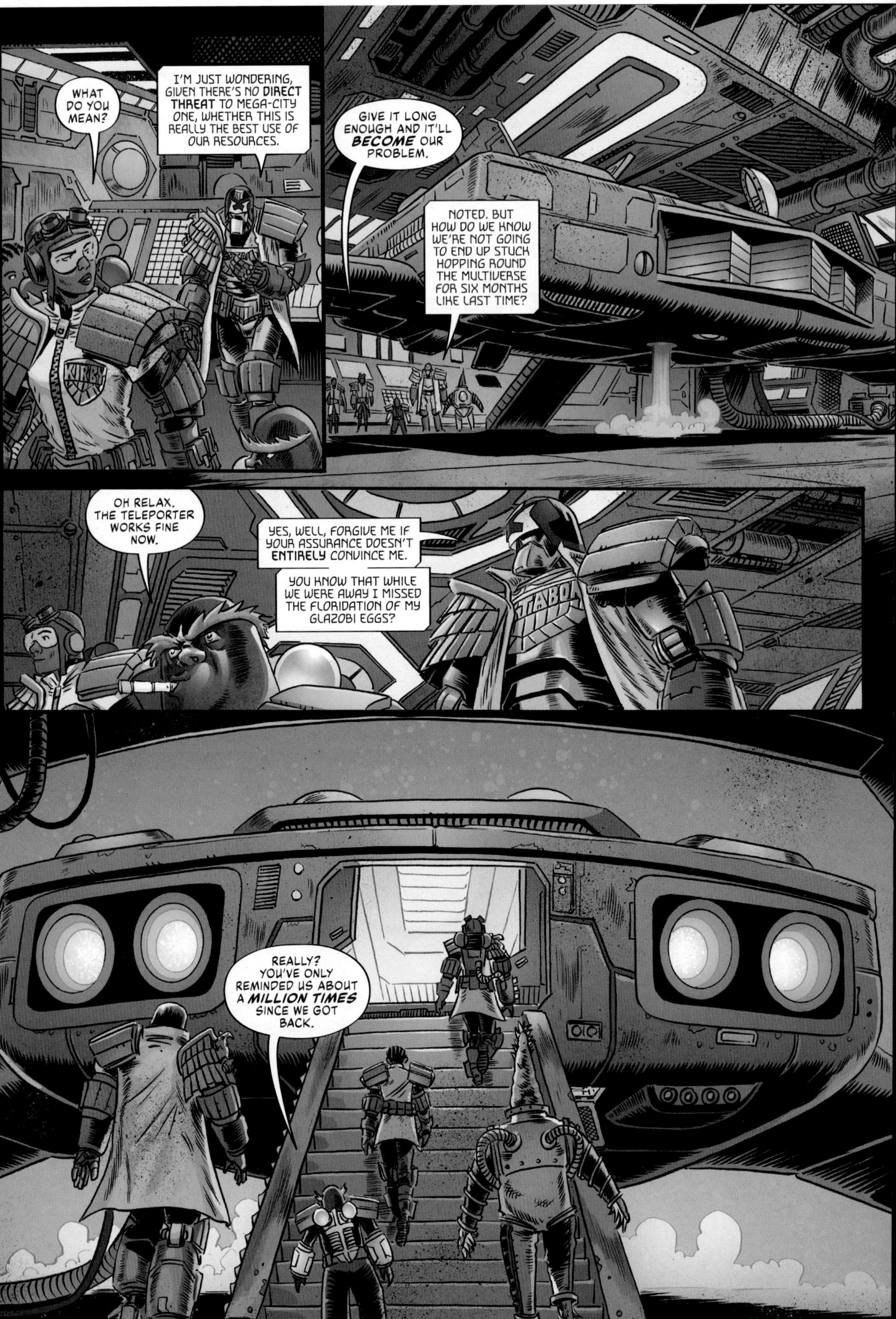
WHAT DO YOU MEAN?
I'M JUST WONDERING, GIVEN THERE'S NO DIRECT THREAT TO MEGA-CITY ONE, WHETHER THIS IS REALLY THE BEST USE OF OUR RESOURCES.
GIVE IT LONG ENOUGH AND IT'LL BECOME OUR PROBLEM.
NOTED. BUT HOW DO WE KNOW WE'RE NOT GOING TO END UP STUCK HOPPING ROUND THE MULTIVERSE FOR SIX MONTHS LIKE LAST TIME?
OH RELAX. THE TELEPORTER WORKS FINE NOW.
YES, WELL, FORGIVE ME IF YOUR ASSURANCE DOESN'T ENTIRELY CONVINCE ME.
YOU KNOW THAT WHILE WE WERE AWAY I MISSED THE FLORIDATION OF MY GLAZOBI EGGS?
REALLY? YOU'VE ONLY REMINDED US ABOUT A MILLION TIMES SINCE WE GOT BACK.

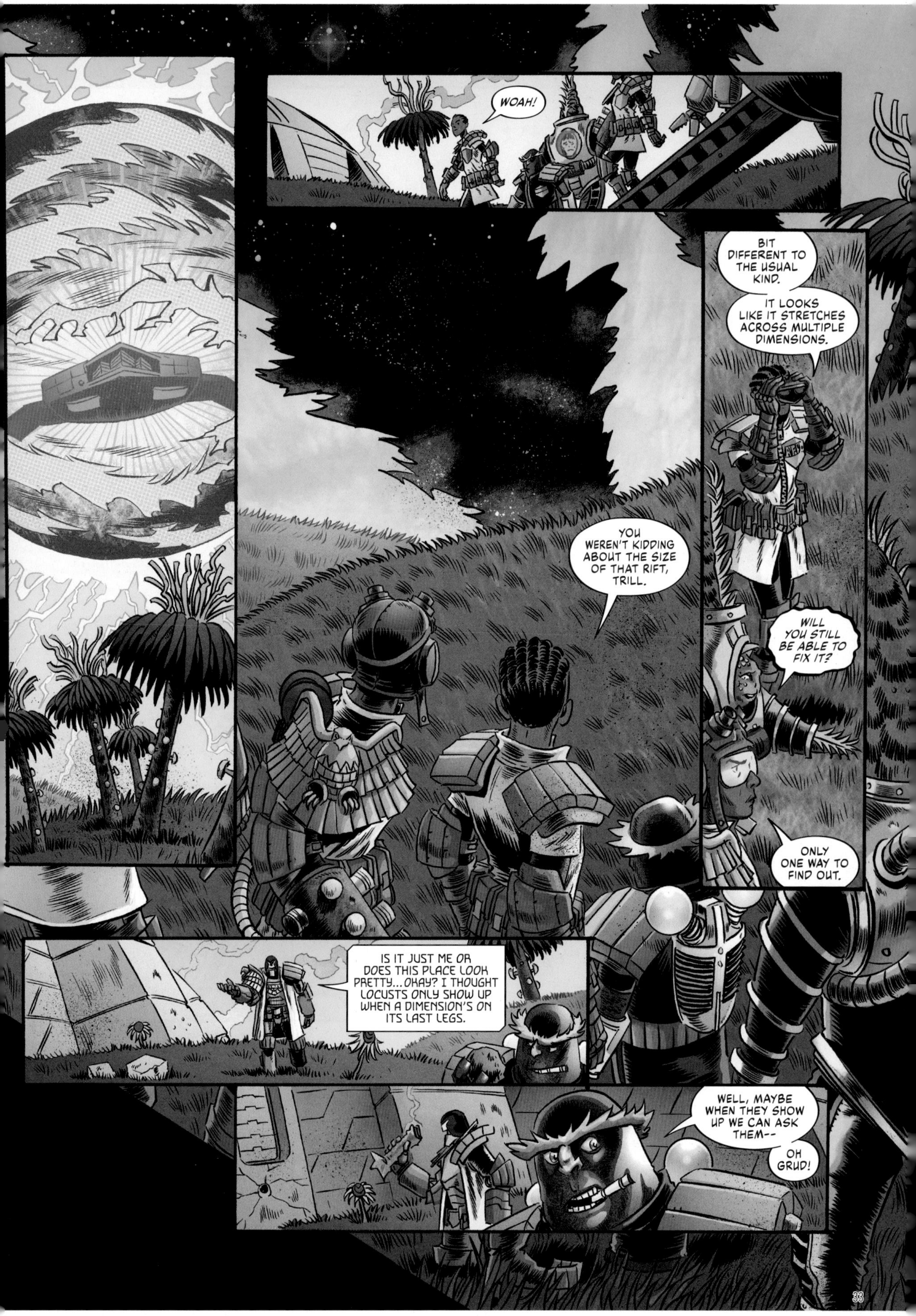
WOAH!
BIT DIFFERENT TO THE USUAL KIND.
IT LOOKS LIKE IT STRETCHES ACROSS MULTIPLE DIMENSIONS.
YOU WEREN'T KIDDING ABOUT THE SIZE OF THAT RIFT, TRILL.
WILL YOU STILL BE ABLE TO FIX IT?
ONLY ONE WAY TO FIND OUT.
IS IT JUST ME OR DOES THIS PLACE LOOK PRETTY...OKAY? I THOUGHT LOCUSTS ONLY SHOW UP WHEN A DIMENSION'S ON ITS LAST LEGS.
WELL, MAYBE WHEN THEY SHOW UP WE CAN ASK THEM--
OH GRUD!

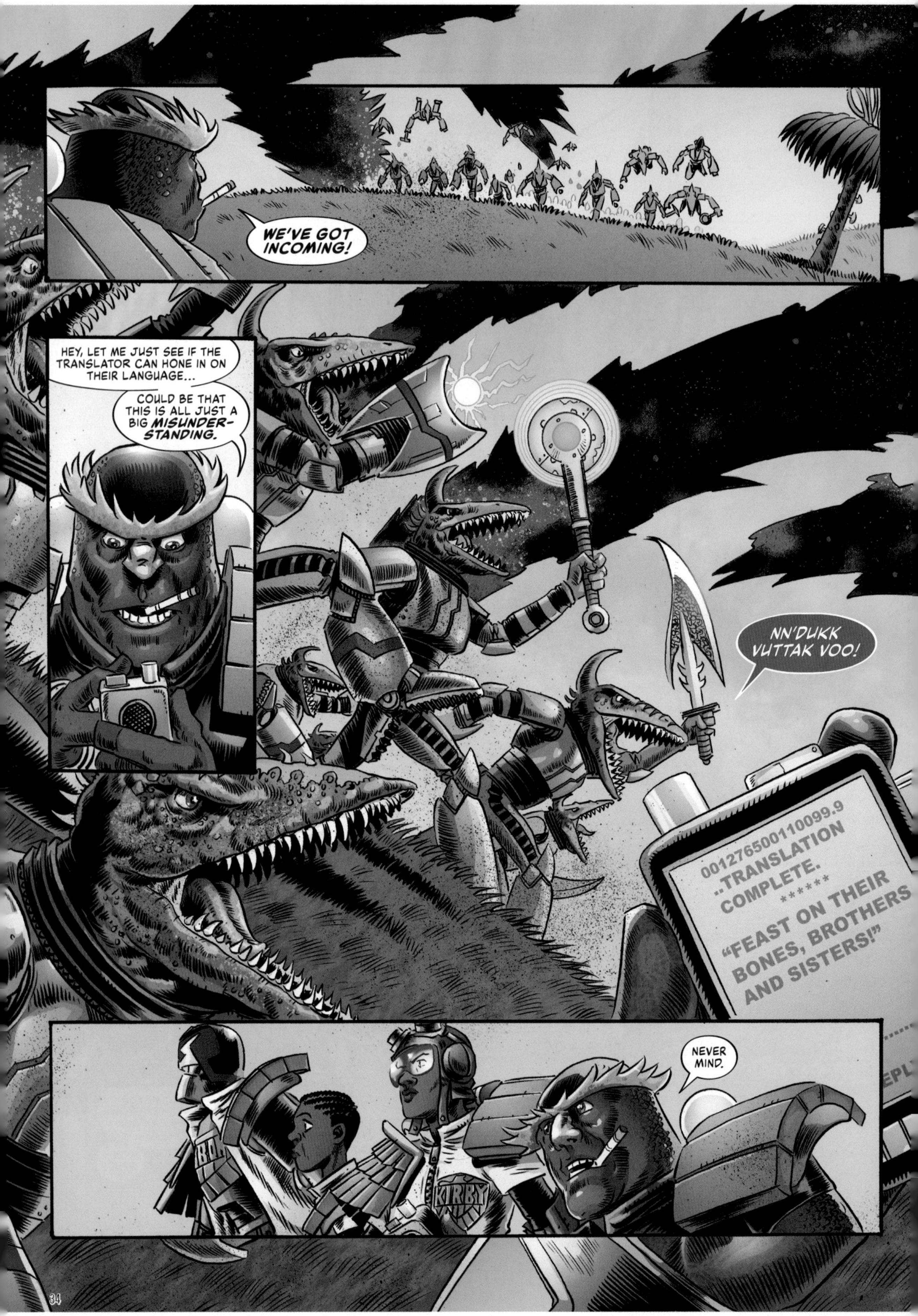
WE'VE GOT INCOMING!
HEY, LET ME JUST SEE IF THE TRANSLATOR CAN HONE IN ON THEIR LANGUAGE...
COULD BE THAT THIS IS ALL JUST A BIG MISUNDER-STANDING.
NN'DUKK VUTTAK VOO!
001276500110099.9
..TRANSLATION COMPLETE.
******
"FEAST ON THEIR BONES, BROTHERS AND SISTERS!"
NEVER MIND.
KIRBY

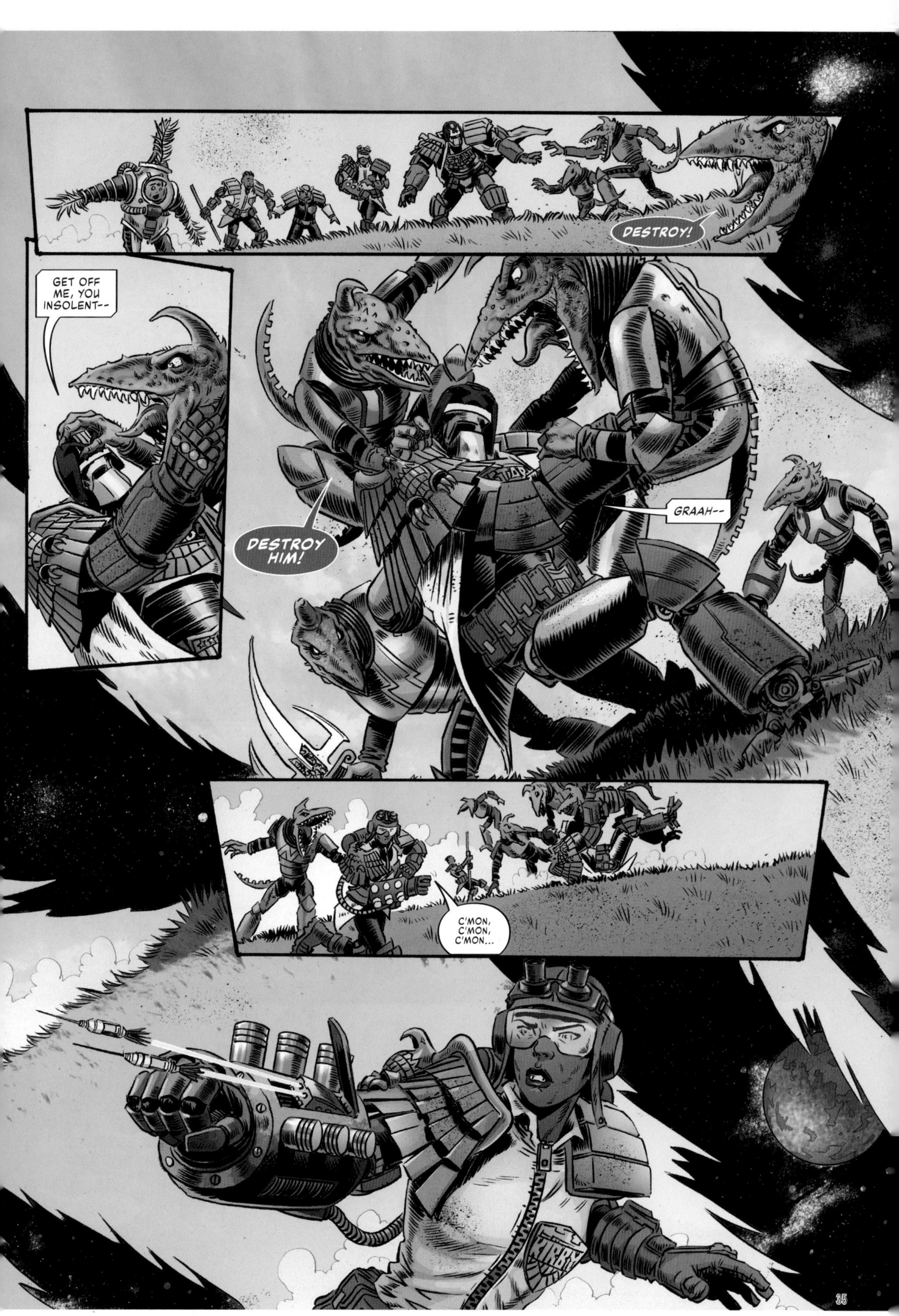
DESTROY!
GET OFF ME, YOU INSOLENT--
DESTROY HIM!
GRAAH--
C'MON, C'MON, C'MON...

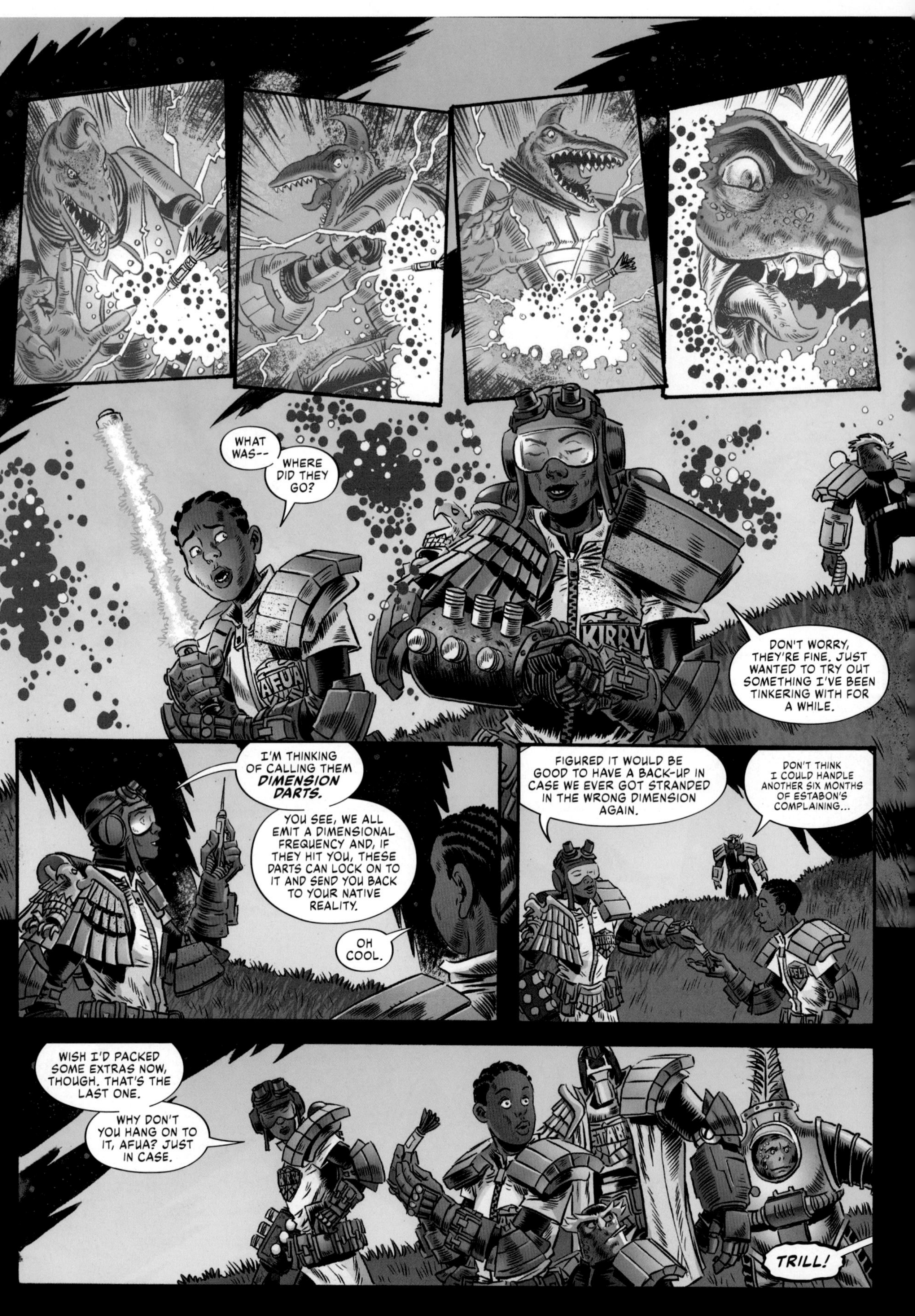

WHAT WAS--
WHERE DID THEY GO?
DON'T WORRY, THEY'RE FINE. JUST WANTED TO TRY OUT SOMETHING I'VE BEEN TINKERING WITH FOR A WHILE.
I'M THINKING OF CALLING THEM *DIMENSION DARTS.*
YOU SEE, WE ALL EMIT A DIMENSIONAL FREQUENCY AND, IF THEY HIT YOU, THESE DARTS CAN LOCK ON TO IT AND SEND YOU BACK TO YOUR NATIVE REALITY.
OH COOL.
FIGURED IT WOULD BE GOOD TO HAVE A BACK-UP IN CASE WE EVER GOT STRANDED IN THE WRONG DIMENSION AGAIN.
DON'T THINK I COULD HANDLE ANOTHER SIX MONTHS OF ESTABON'S COMPLAINING...
WISH I'D PACKED SOME EXTRAS NOW, THOUGH. THAT'S THE LAST ONE.
WHY DON'T YOU HANG ON TO IT, AFUA? JUST IN CASE.
TRILL!

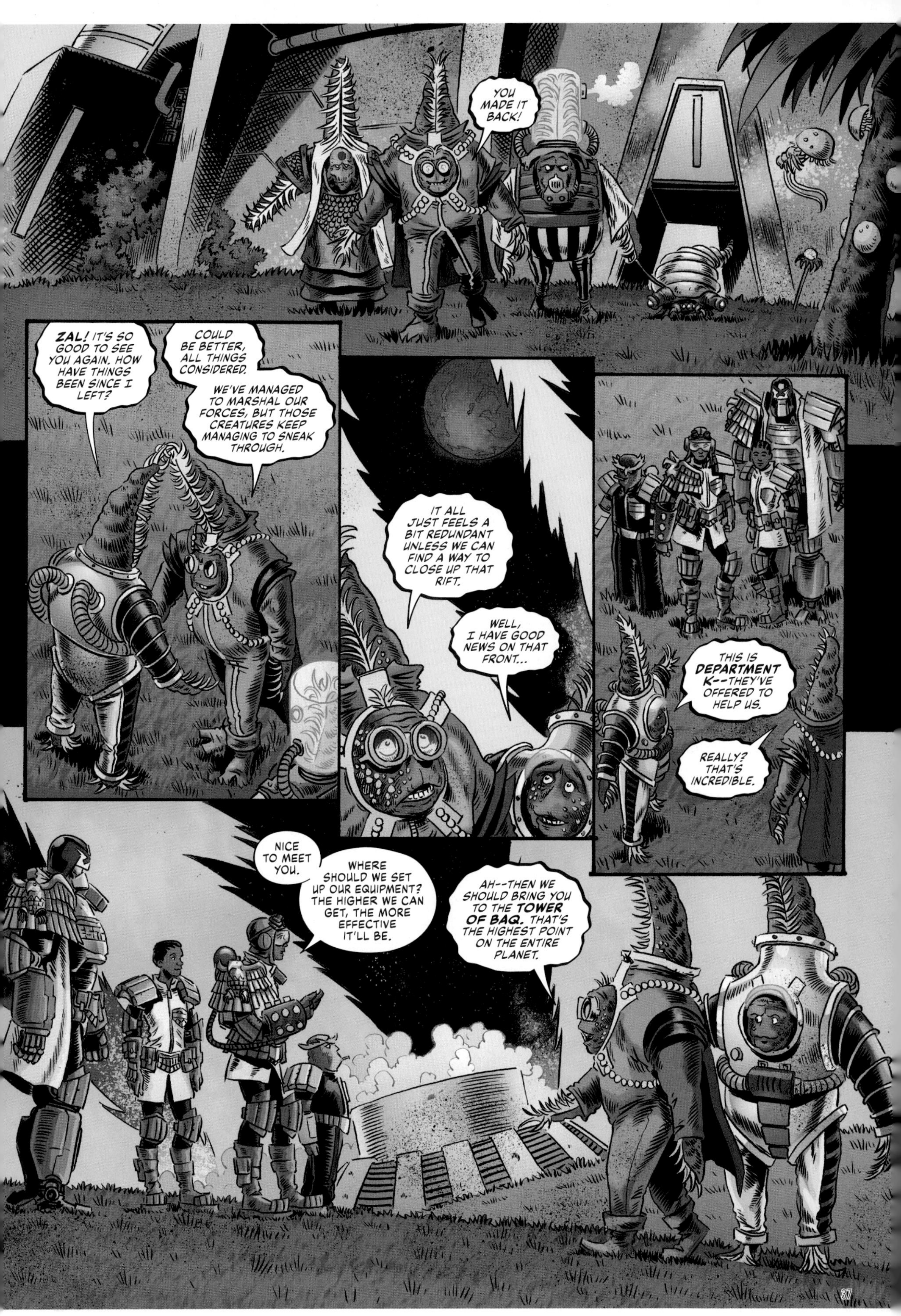
YOU MADE IT BACK!
ZAL! IT'S SO GOOD TO SEE YOU AGAIN. HOW HAVE THINGS BEEN SINCE I LEFT?
COULD BE BETTER, ALL THINGS CONSIDERED.
WE'VE MANAGED TO MARSHAL OUR FORCES, BUT THOSE CREATURES KEEP MANAGING TO SNEAK THROUGH.
IT ALL JUST FEELS A BIT REDUNDANT UNLESS WE CAN FIND A WAY TO CLOSE UP THAT RIFT.
WELL, I HAVE GOOD NEWS ON THAT FRONT...
THIS IS DEPARTMENT K--THEY'VE OFFERED TO HELP US.
REALLY? THAT'S INCREDIBLE.
NICE TO MEET YOU.
WHERE SHOULD WE SET UP OUR EQUIPMENT? THE HIGHER WE CAN GET, THE MORE EFFECTIVE IT'LL BE.
AH--THEN WE SHOULD BRING YOU TO THE TOWER OF BAQ. THAT'S THE HIGHEST POINT ON THE ENTIRE PLANET.

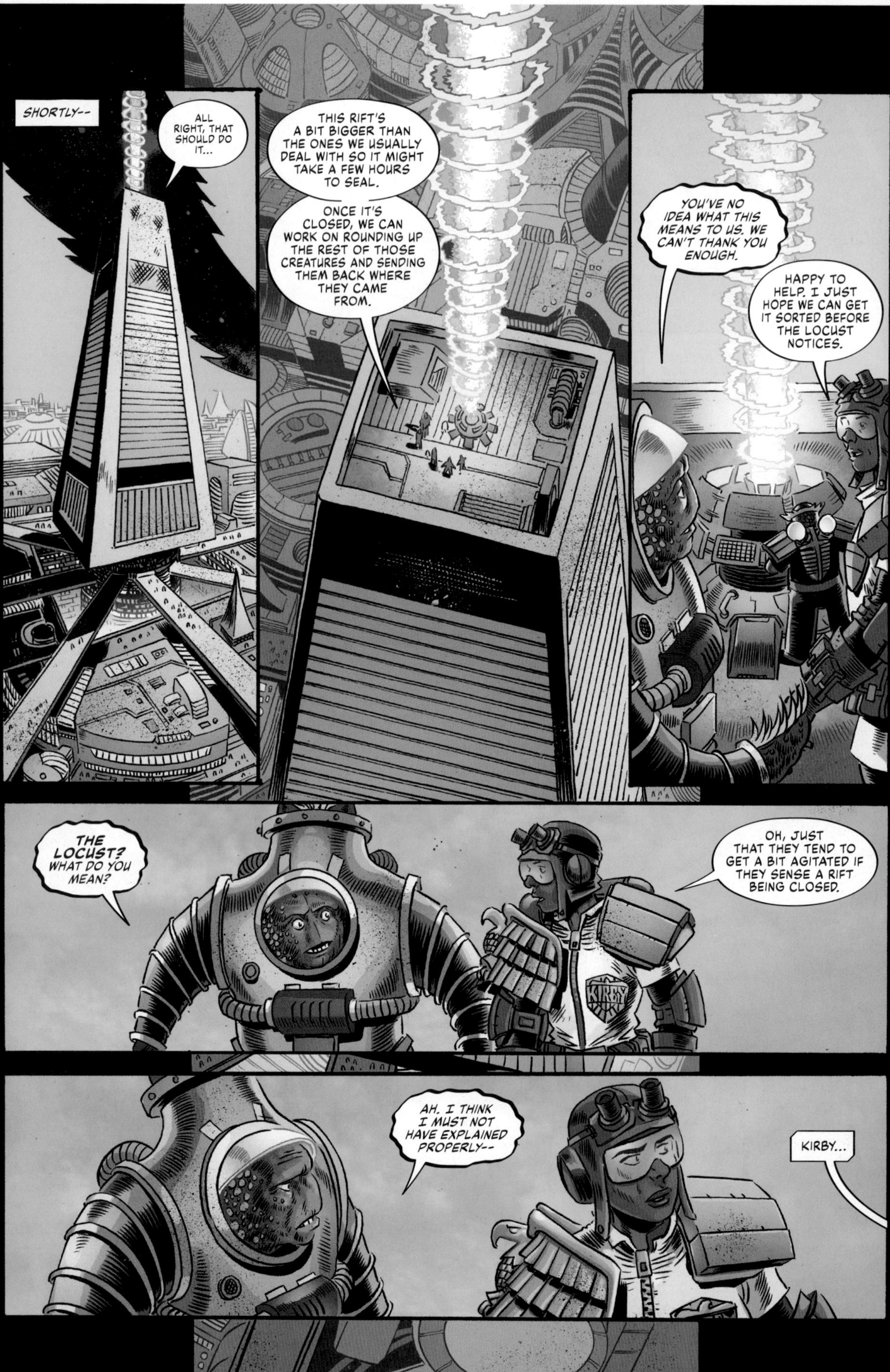
SHORTLY--
ALL RIGHT, THAT SHOULD DO IT...
THIS RIFT'S A BIT BIGGER THAN THE ONES WE USUALLY DEAL WITH SO IT MIGHT TAKE A FEW HOURS TO SEAL.
ONCE IT'S CLOSED, WE CAN WORK ON ROUNDING UP THE REST OF THOSE CREATURES AND SENDING THEM BACK WHERE THEY CAME FROM.
YOU'VE NO IDEA WHAT THIS MEANS TO US. WE CAN'T THANK YOU ENOUGH.
HAPPY TO HELP. I JUST HOPE WE CAN GET IT SORTED BEFORE THE LOCUST NOTICES.
THE LOCUST? WHAT DO YOU MEAN?
OH, JUST THAT THEY TEND TO GET A BIT AGITATED IF THEY SENSE A RIFT BEING CLOSED.
KIRBY
AH. I THINK I MUST NOT HAVE EXPLAINED PROPERLY--
KIRBY...

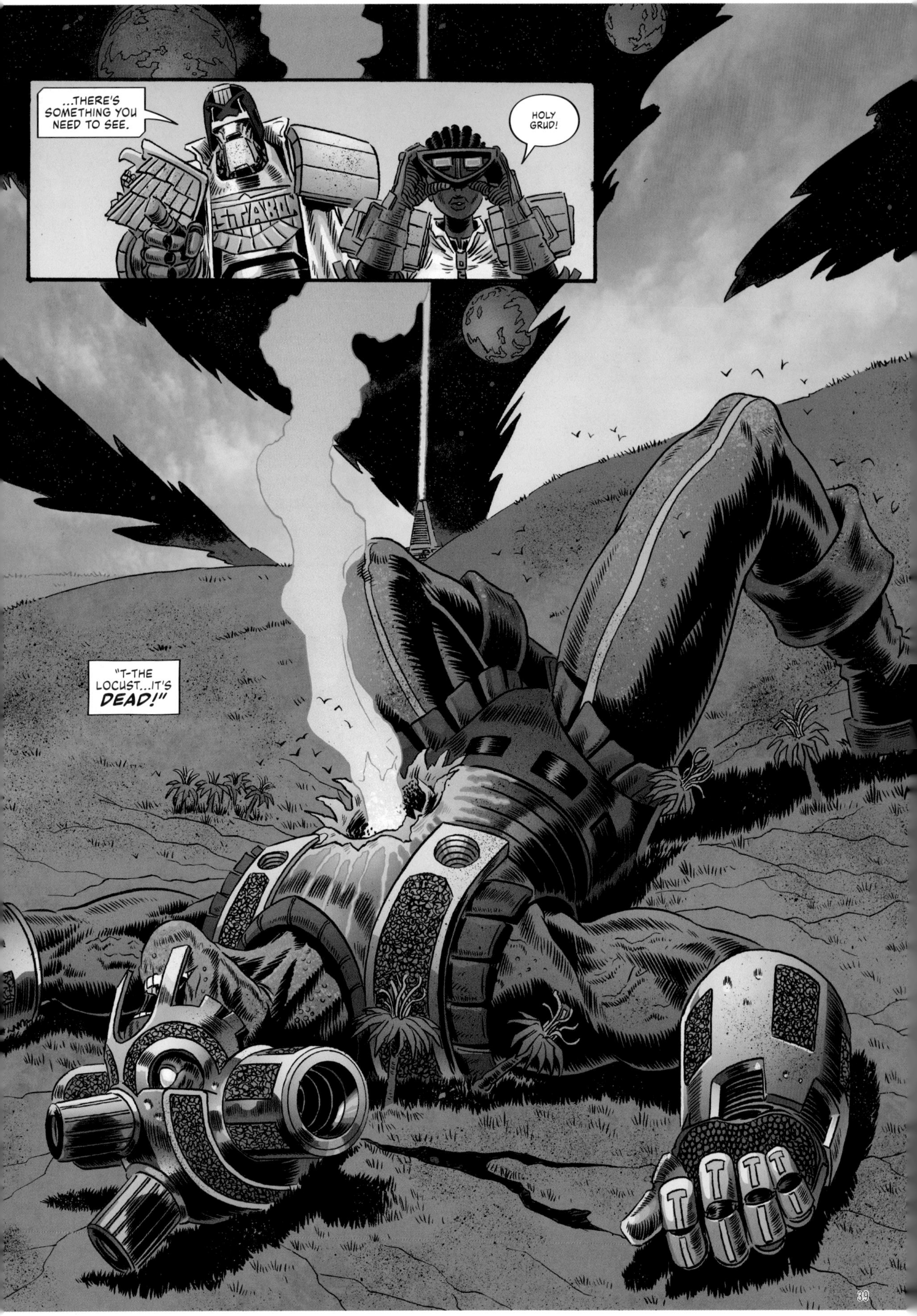

...THERE'S SOMETHING YOU NEED TO SEE.
HOLY GRUD!
"T-THE LOCUST...IT'S DEAD!"

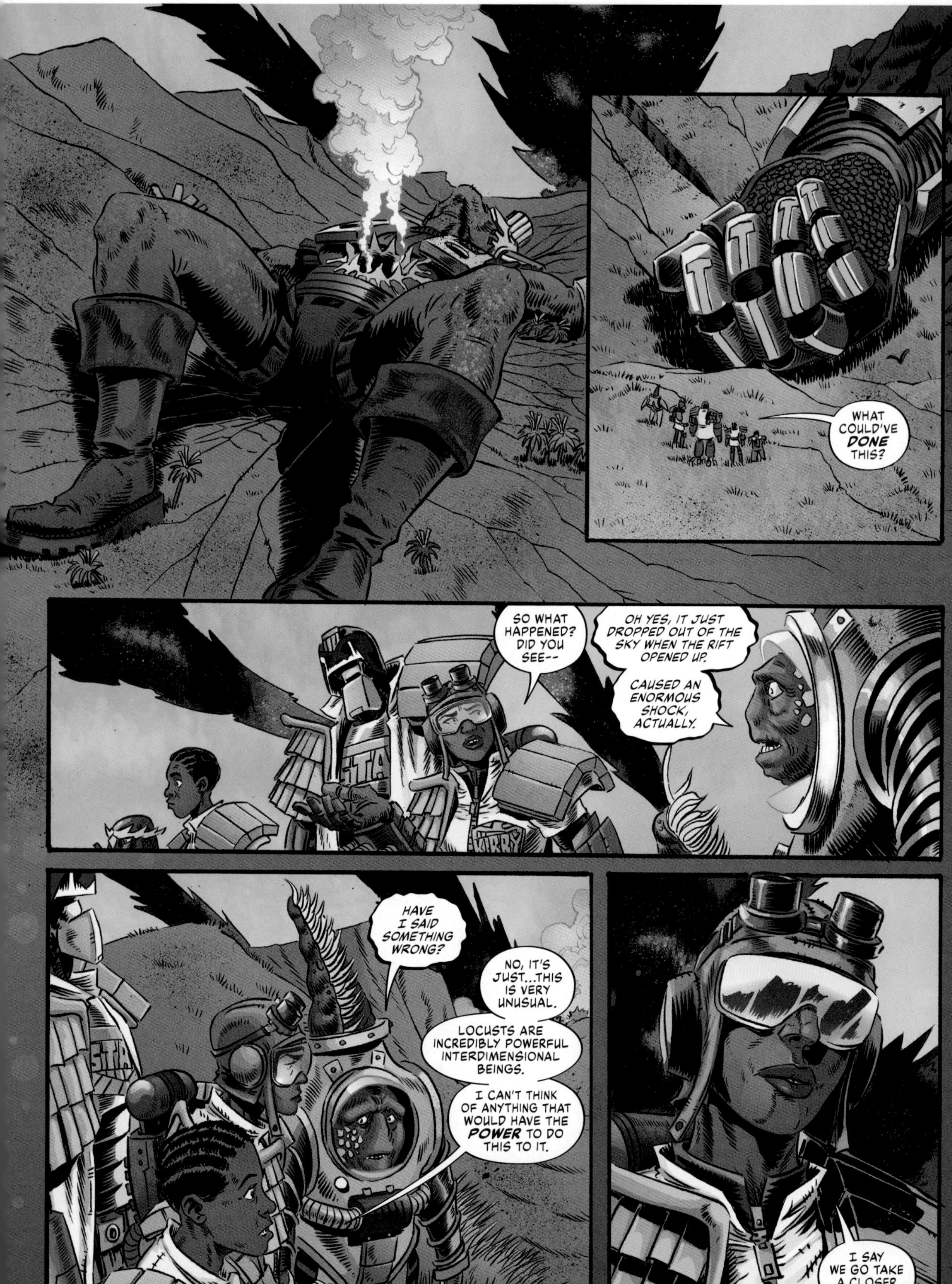
WHAT COULD'VE DONE THIS?
SO WHAT HAPPENED? DID YOU SEE--
OH YES, IT JUST DROPPED OUT OF THE SKY WHEN THE RIFT OPENED UP.
CAUSED AN ENORMOUS SHOCK, ACTUALLY.
HAVE I SAID SOMETHING WRONG?
NO, IT'S JUST...THIS IS VERY UNUSUAL.
LOCUSTS ARE INCREDIBLY POWERFUL INTERDIMENSIONAL BEINGS.
I CAN'T THINK OF ANYTHING THAT WOULD HAVE THE POWER TO DO THIS TO IT.
I SAY WE GO TAKE A CLOSER LOOK.

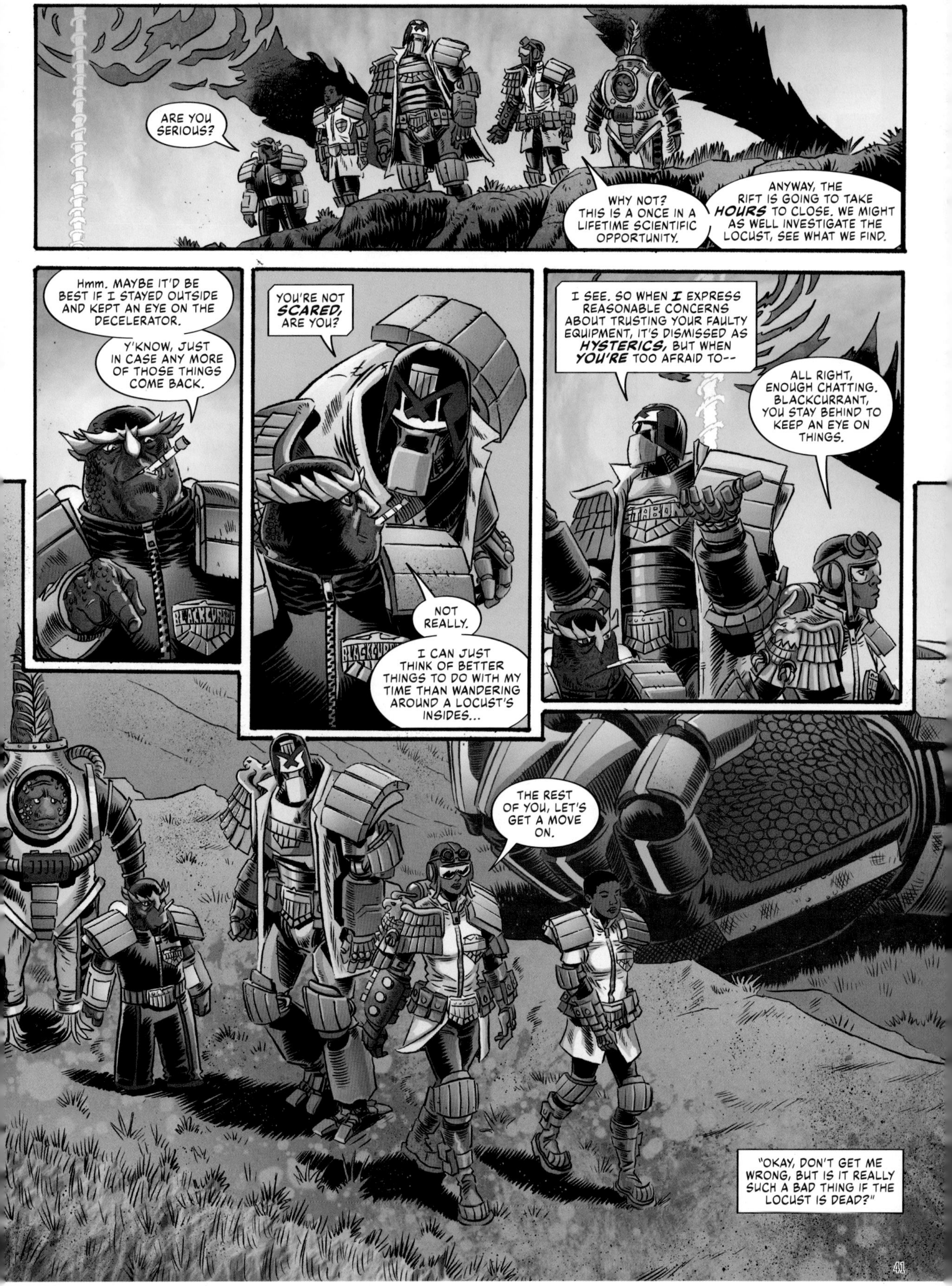

ARE YOU SERIOUS?
WHY NOT? THIS IS A ONCE IN A LIFETIME SCIENTIFIC OPPORTUNITY.
ANYWAY, THE RIFT IS GOING TO TAKE HOURS TO CLOSE. WE MIGHT AS WELL INVESTIGATE THE LOCUST, SEE WHAT WE FIND.
Hmm. MAYBE IT'D BE BEST IF I STAYED OUTSIDE AND KEPT AN EYE ON THE DECELERATOR.
Y'KNOW, JUST IN CASE ANY MORE OF THOSE THINGS COME BACK.
BLACKCURRANT
YOU'RE NOT SCARED, ARE YOU?
NOT REALLY.
I CAN JUST THINK OF BETTER THINGS TO DO WITH MY TIME THAN WANDERING AROUND A LOCUST'S INSIDES...
I SEE. SO WHEN I EXPRESS REASONABLE CONCERNS ABOUT TRUSTING YOUR FAULTY EQUIPMENT, IT'S DISMISSED AS HYSTERICS, BUT WHEN YOU'RE TOO AFRAID TO--
ALL RIGHT, ENOUGH CHATTING. BLACKCURRANT, YOU STAY BEHIND TO KEEP AN EYE ON THINGS.
THE REST OF YOU, LET'S GET A MOVE ON.
"OKAY, DON'T GET ME WRONG, BUT IS IT REALLY SUCH A BAD THING IF THE LOCUST IS DEAD?"

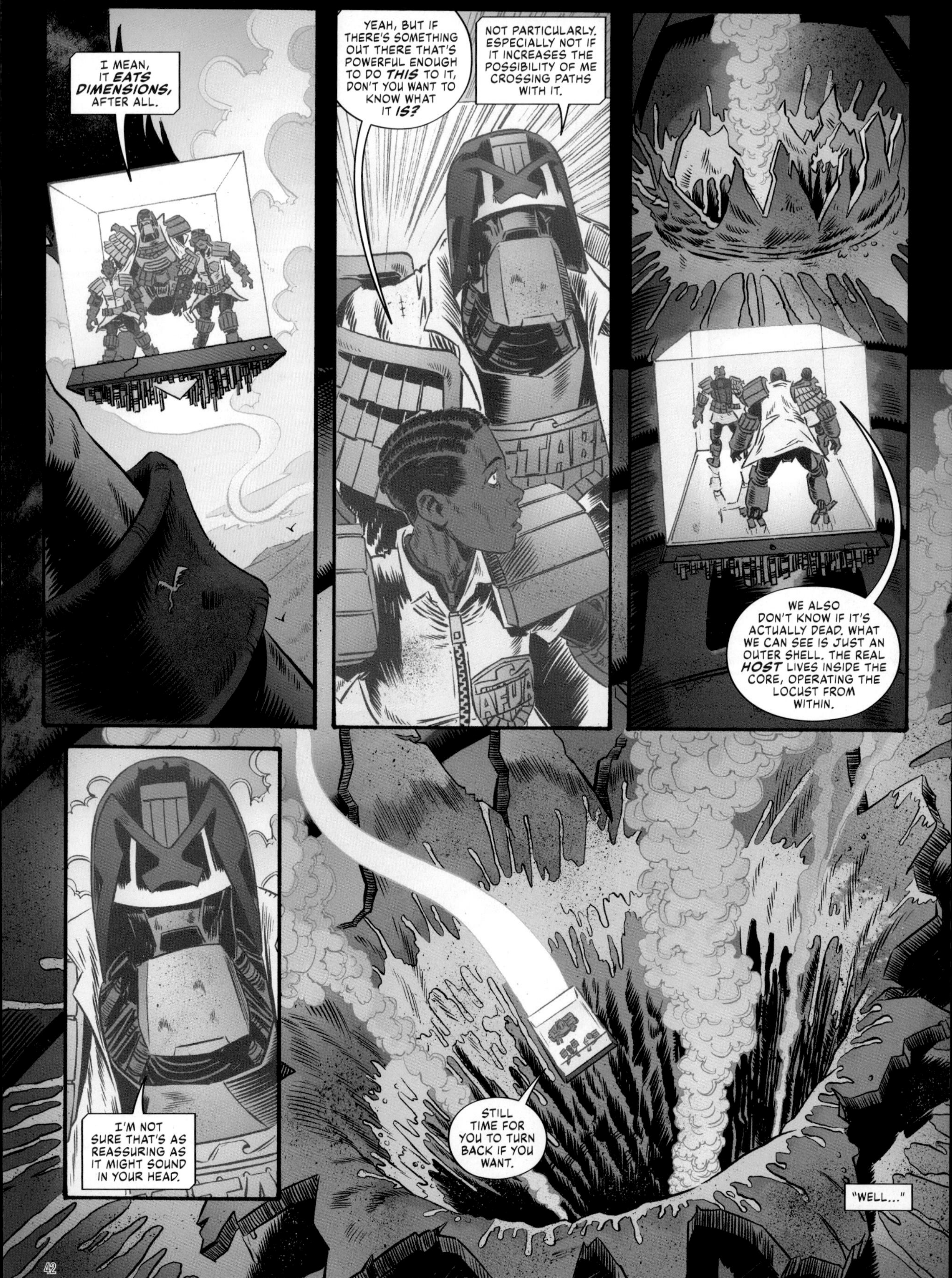
I MEAN, IT EATS DIMENSIONS, AFTER ALL.
YEAH, BUT IF THERE'S SOMETHING OUT THERE THAT'S POWERFUL ENOUGH TO DO THIS TO IT, DON'T YOU WANT TO KNOW WHAT IT IS?
NOT PARTICULARLY. ESPECIALLY NOT IF IT INCREASES THE POSSIBILITY OF ME CROSSING PATHS WITH IT.
TAB
AFUA
WE ALSO DON'T KNOW IF IT'S ACTUALLY DEAD. WHAT WE CAN SEE IS JUST AN OUTER SHELL. THE REAL HOST LIVES INSIDE THE CORE, OPERATING THE LOCUST FROM WITHIN.
I'M NOT SURE THAT'S AS REASSURING AS IT MIGHT SOUND IN YOUR HEAD.
STILL TIME FOR YOU TO TURN BACK IF YOU WANT.
"WELL..."

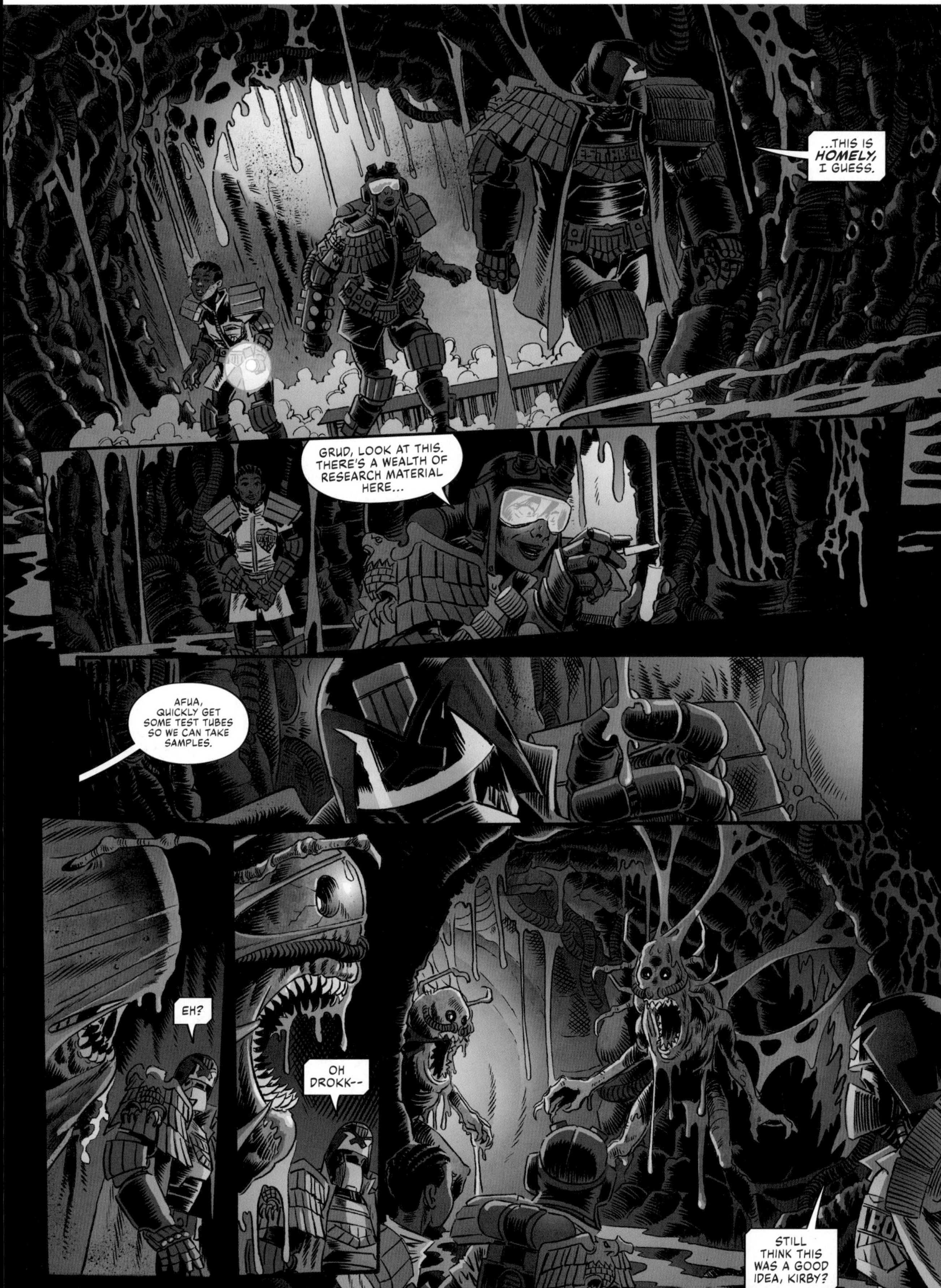
...THIS IS HOMELY, I GUESS.
GRUD, LOOK AT THIS. THERE'S A WEALTH OF RESEARCH MATERIAL HERE...
AFUA, QUICKLY GET SOME TEST TUBES SO WE CAN TAKE SAMPLES.
EH?
OH DROKK--
STILL THINK THIS WAS A GOOD IDEA, KIRBY?

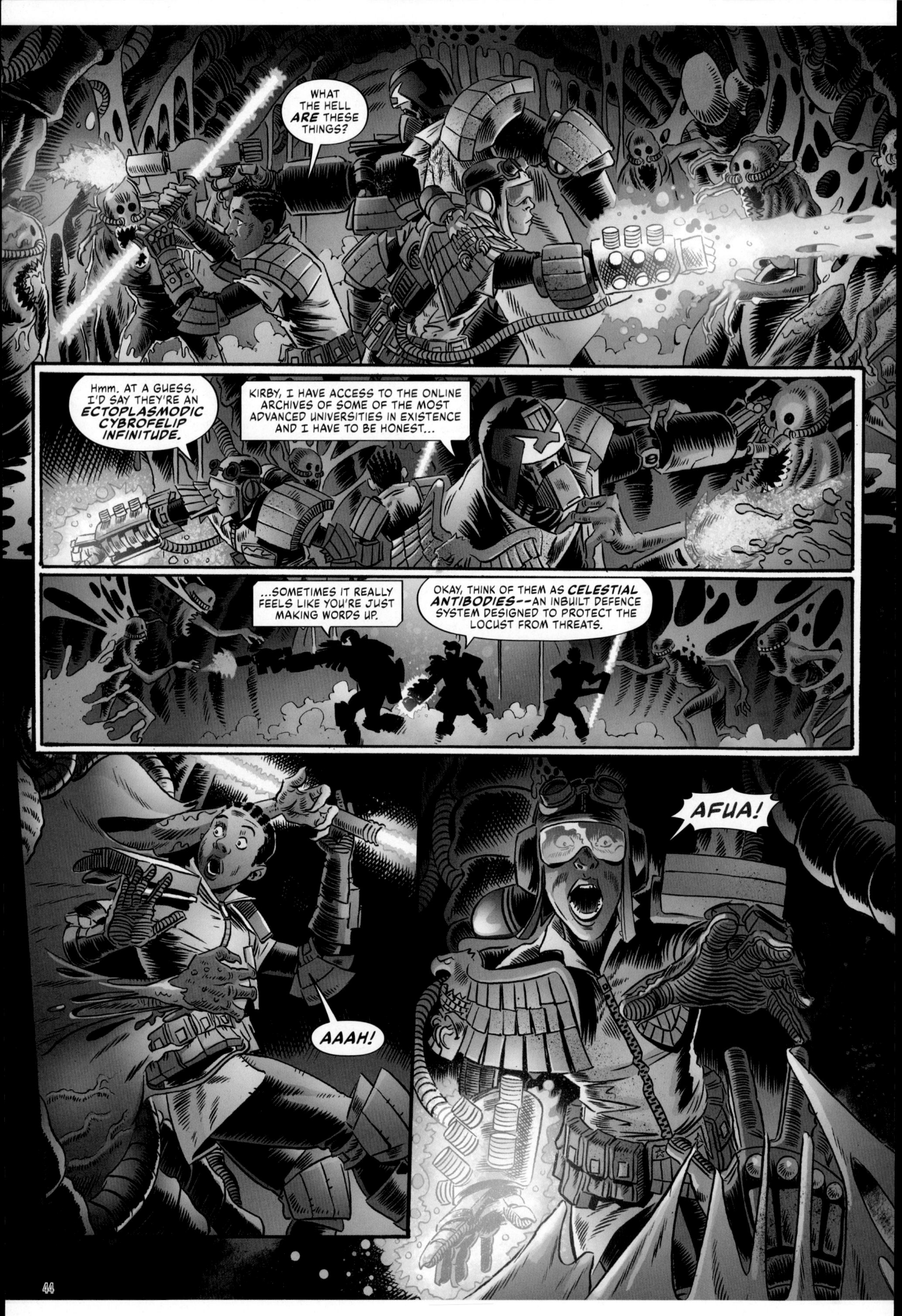

WHAT THE HELL ARE THESE THINGS?
Hmm. AT A GUESS, I'D SAY THEY'RE AN ECTOPLASMODIC CYBROFELIP INFINITUDE.
KIRBY, I HAVE ACCESS TO THE ONLINE ARCHIVES OF SOME OF THE MOST ADVANCED UNIVERSITIES IN EXISTENCE AND I HAVE TO BE HONEST...
...SOMETIMES IT REALLY FEELS LIKE YOU'RE JUST MAKING WORDS UP.
OKAY, THINK OF THEM AS CELESTIAL ANTIBODIES--AN INBUILT DEFENCE SYSTEM DESIGNED TO PROTECT THE LOCUST FROM THREATS.
AFUA!
AAAH!

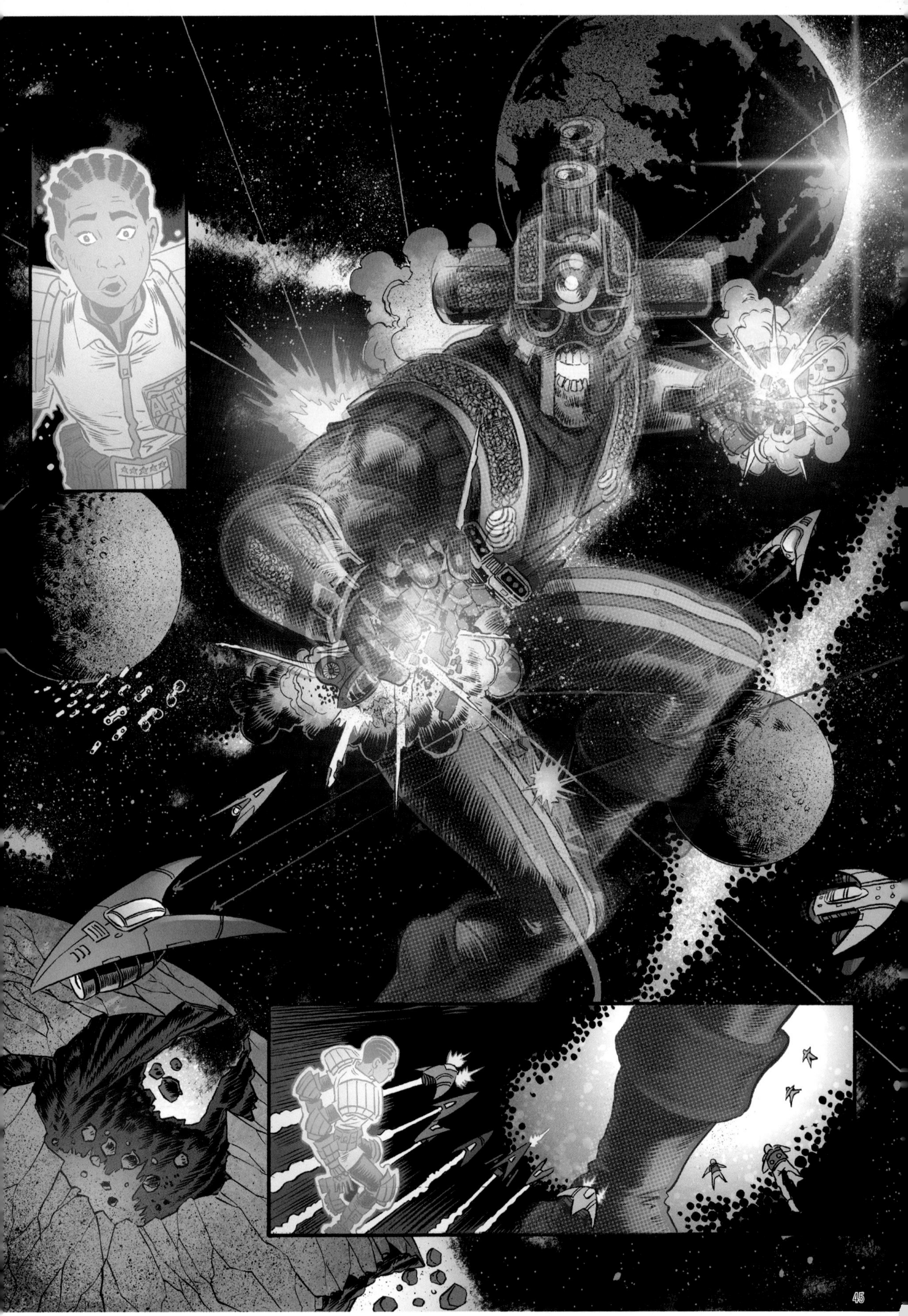

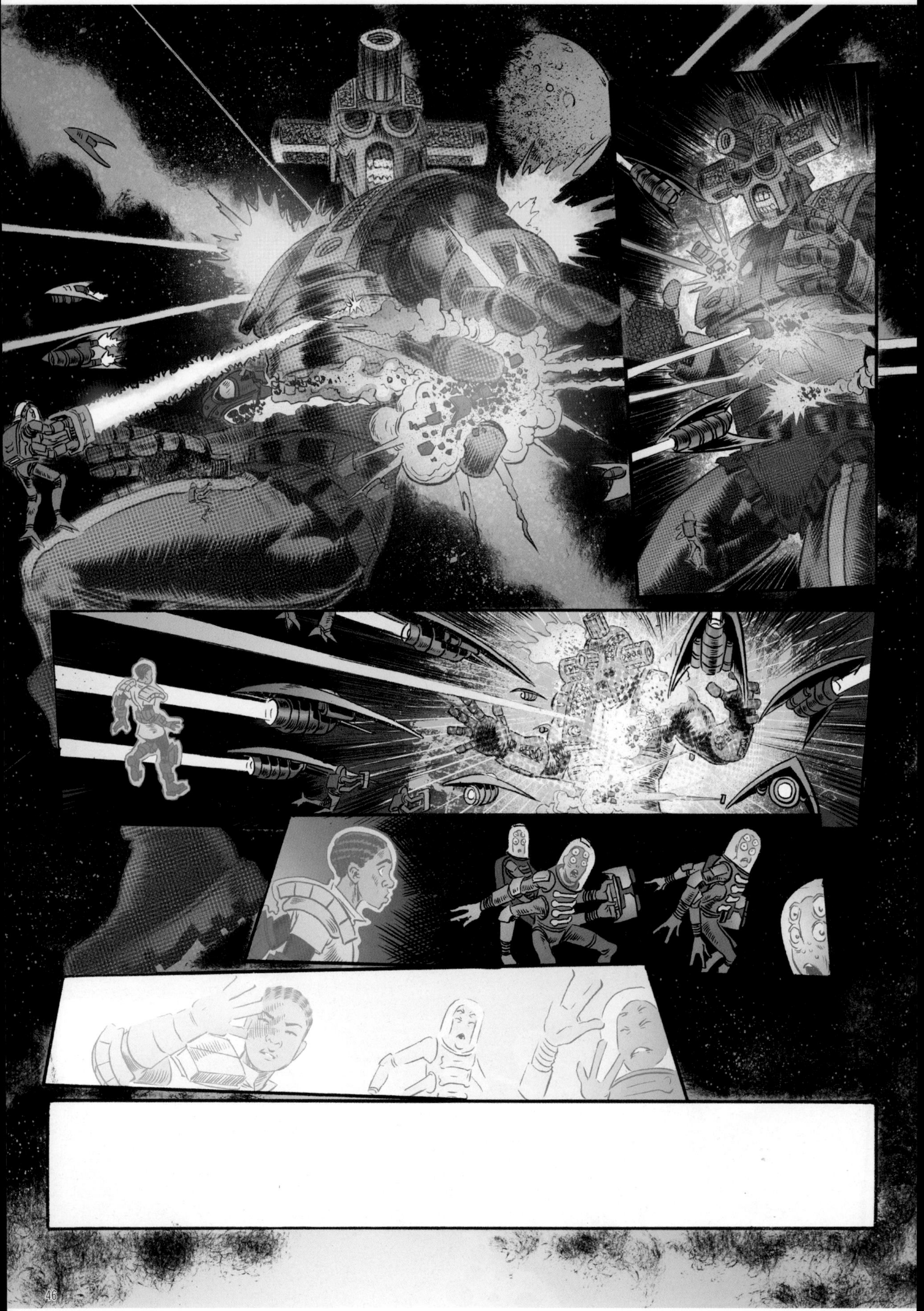

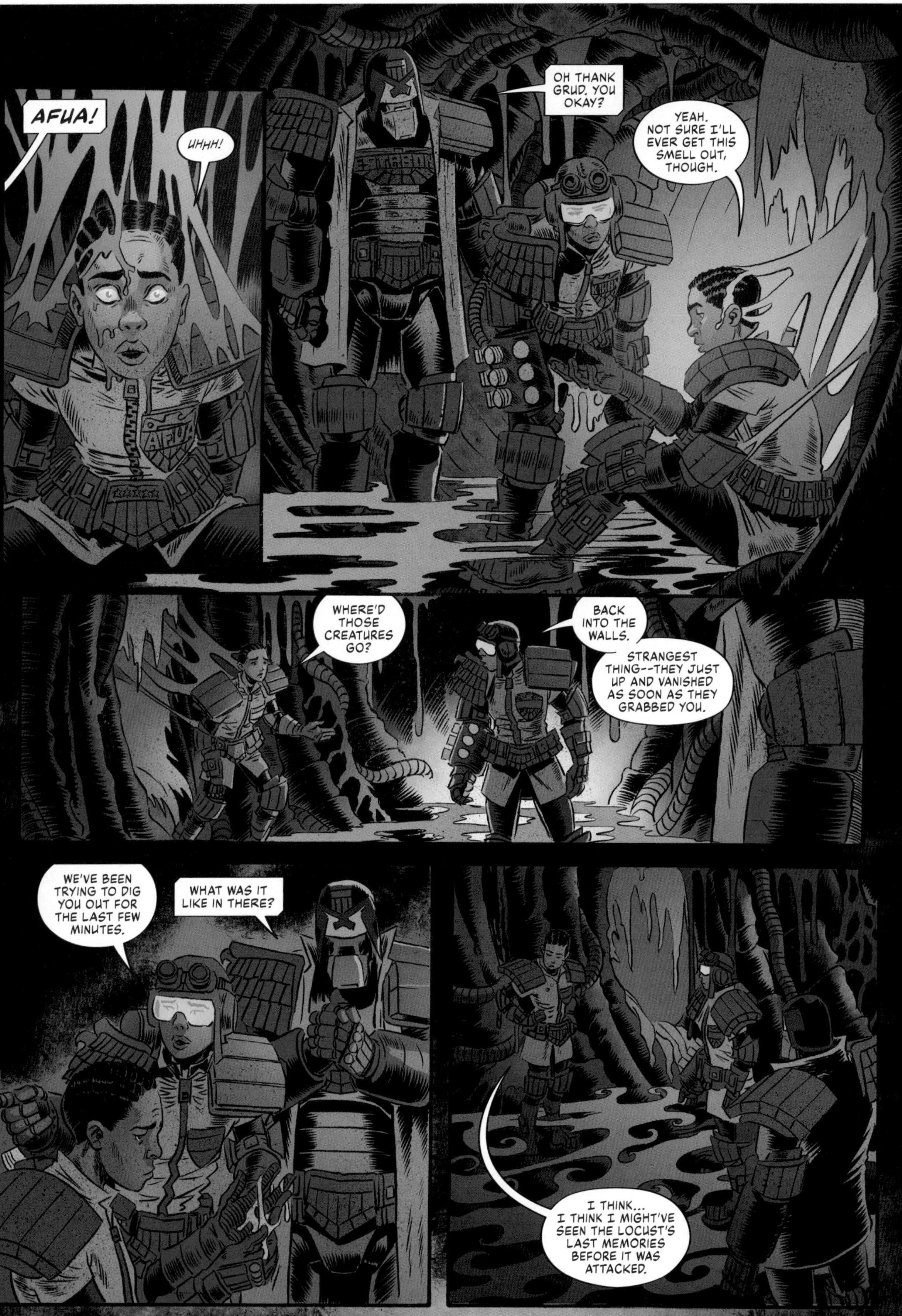
AFUA!
UHHH!
OH THANK GRUD. YOU OKAY?
YEAH. NOT SURE I'LL EVER GET THIS SMELL OUT, THOUGH.
WHERE'D THOSE CREATURES GO?
BACK INTO THE WALLS.
STRANGEST THING--THEY JUST UP AND VANISHED AS SOON AS THEY GRABBED YOU.
WE'VE BEEN TRYING TO DIG YOU OUT FOR THE LAST FEW MINUTES.
WHAT WAS IT LIKE IN THERE?
I THINK... I THINK I MIGHT'VE SEEN THE LOCUST'S LAST MEMORIES BEFORE IT WAS ATTACKED.

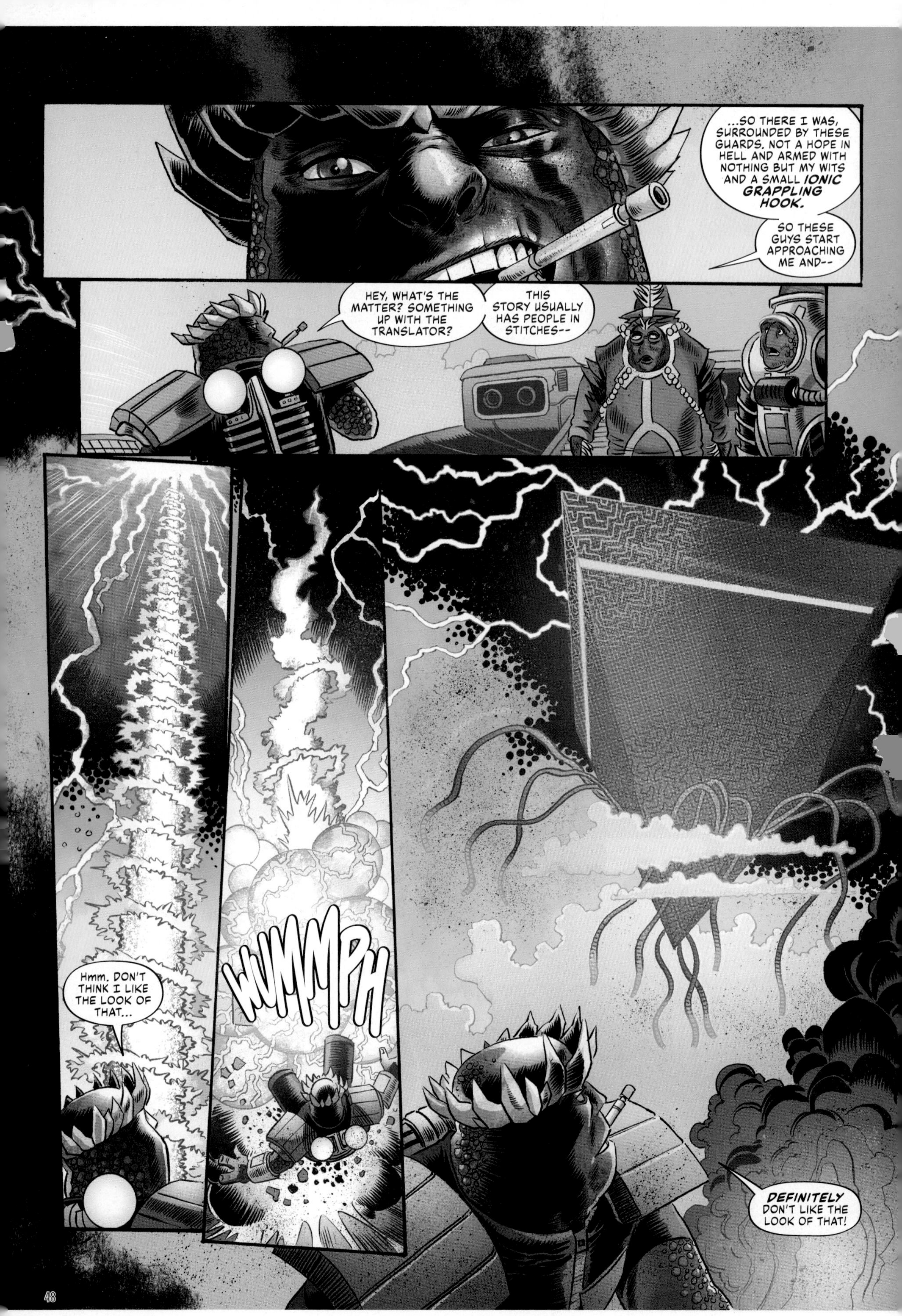
...SO THERE I WAS, SURROUNDED BY THESE GUARDS. NOT A HOPE IN HELL AND ARMED WITH NOTHING BUT MY WITS AND A SMALL IONIC GRAPPLING HOOK.
SO THESE GUYS START APPROACHING ME AND--
HEY, WHAT'S THE MATTER? SOMETHING UP WITH THE TRANSLATOR?
THIS STORY USUALLY HAS PEOPLE IN STITCHES--
Hmm. DON'T THINK I LIKE THE LOOK OF THAT...
WUMMPH
DEFINITELY DON'T LIKE THE LOOK OF THAT!

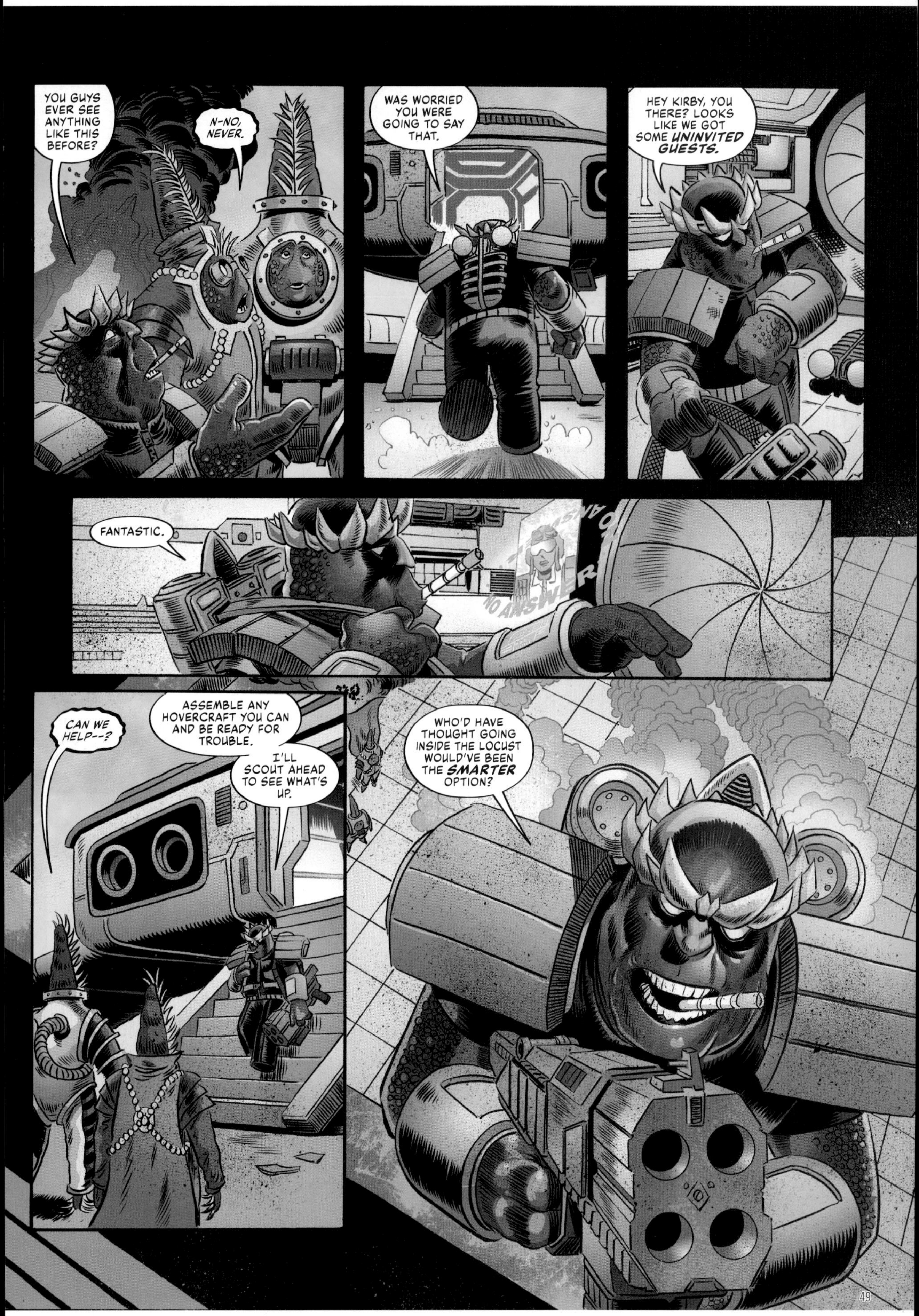

YOU GUYS EVER SEE ANYTHING LIKE THIS BEFORE?
N-NO, NEVER.
WAS WORRIED YOU WERE GOING TO SAY THAT.
HEY KIRBY, YOU THERE? LOOKS LIKE WE GOT SOME *UNINVITED GUESTS.*
FANTASTIC.
NO ANSWER
CAN WE HELP--?
ASSEMBLE ANY HOVERCRAFT YOU CAN AND BE READY FOR TROUBLE.
I'LL SCOUT AHEAD TO SEE WHAT'S UP.
WHO'D HAVE THOUGHT GOING INSIDE THE LOCUST WOULD'VE BEEN THE *SMARTER* OPTION?

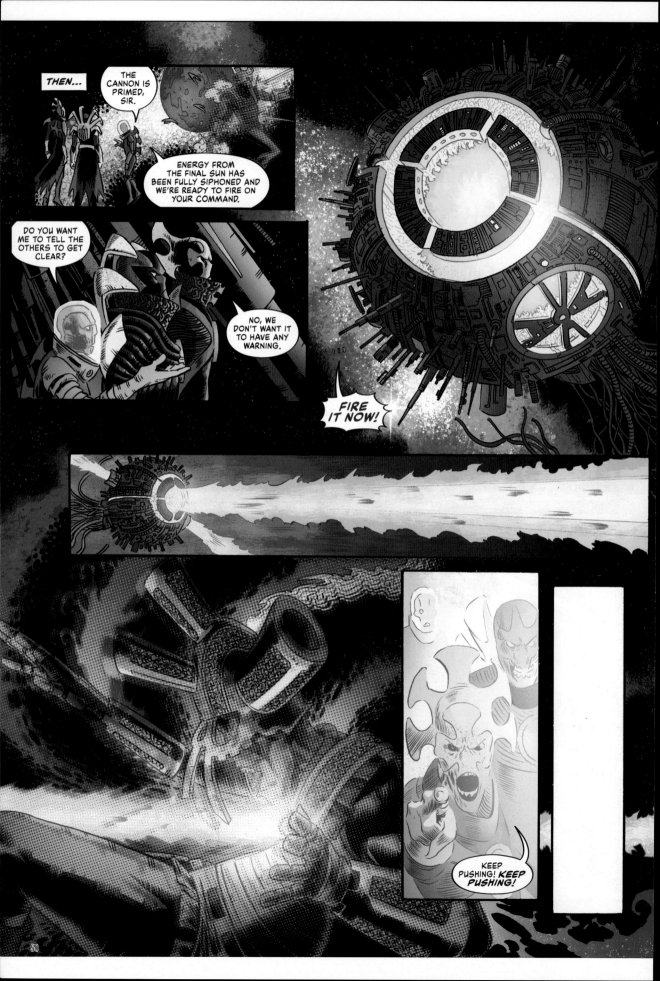

THEN...

THE CANNON IS PRIMED, SIR.

ENERGY FROM THE FINAL SUN HAS BEEN FULLY SIPHONED AND WE'RE READY TO FIRE ON YOUR COMMAND.

DO YOU WANT ME TO TELL THE OTHERS TO GET CLEAR?

NO, WE DON'T WANT IT TO HAVE ANY WARNING.

FIRE IT NOW!

KEEP PUSHING! *KEEP PUSHING!*

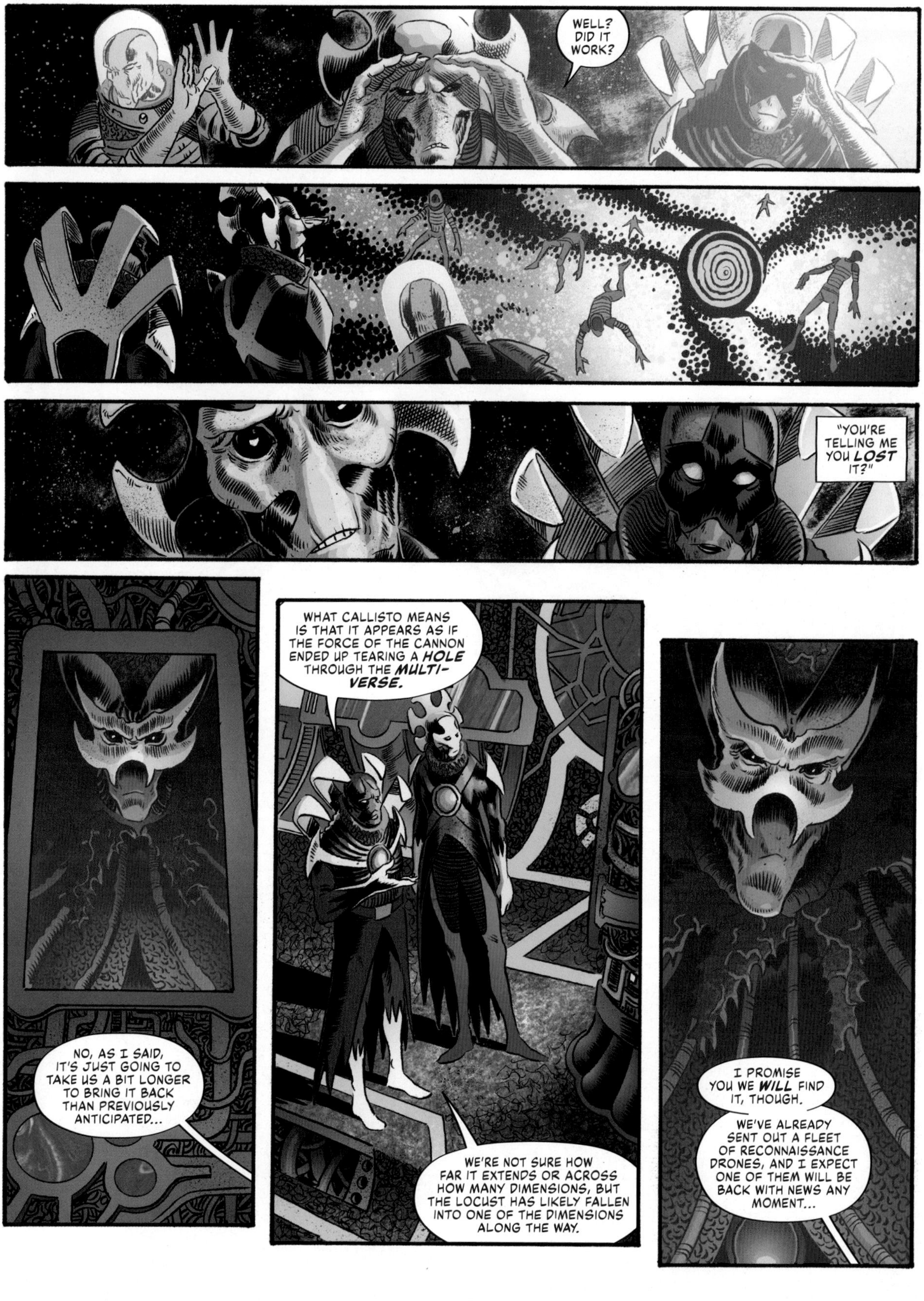
WELL? DID IT WORK?
"YOU'RE TELLING ME YOU LOST IT?"
NO, AS I SAID, IT'S JUST GOING TO TAKE US A BIT LONGER TO BRING IT BACK THAN PREVIOUSLY ANTICIPATED...
WHAT CALLISTO MEANS IS THAT IT APPEARS AS IF THE FORCE OF THE CANNON ENDED UP TEARING A HOLE THROUGH THE MULTI-VERSE.
WE'RE NOT SURE HOW FAR IT EXTENDS OR ACROSS HOW MANY DIMENSIONS, BUT THE LOCUST HAS LIKELY FALLEN INTO ONE OF THE DIMENSIONS ALONG THE WAY.
I PROMISE YOU WE WILL FIND IT, THOUGH.
WE'VE ALREADY SENT OUT A FLEET OF RECONNAISSANCE DRONES, AND I EXPECT ONE OF THEM WILL BE BACK WITH NEWS ANY MOMENT...

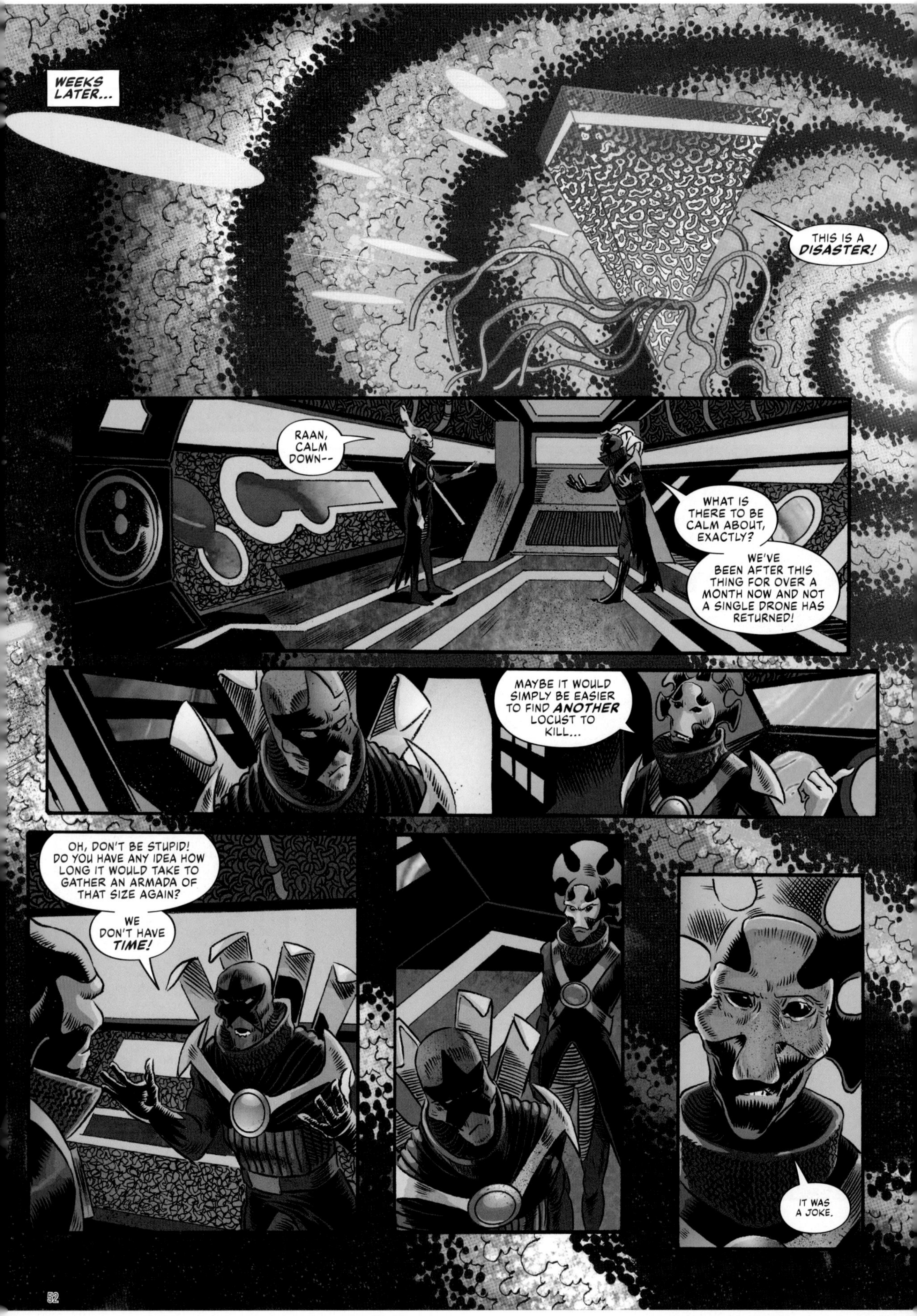
WEEKS LATER...
THIS IS A DISASTER!
RAAN, CALM DOWN--
WHAT IS THERE TO BE CALM ABOUT, EXACTLY?
WE'VE BEEN AFTER THIS THING FOR OVER A MONTH NOW AND NOT A SINGLE DRONE HAS RETURNED!
MAYBE IT WOULD SIMPLY BE EASIER TO FIND ANOTHER LOCUST TO KILL...
OH, DON'T BE STUPID! DO YOU HAVE ANY IDEA HOW LONG IT WOULD TAKE TO GATHER AN ARMADA OF THAT SIZE AGAIN?
WE DON'T HAVE TIME!
IT WAS A JOKE.

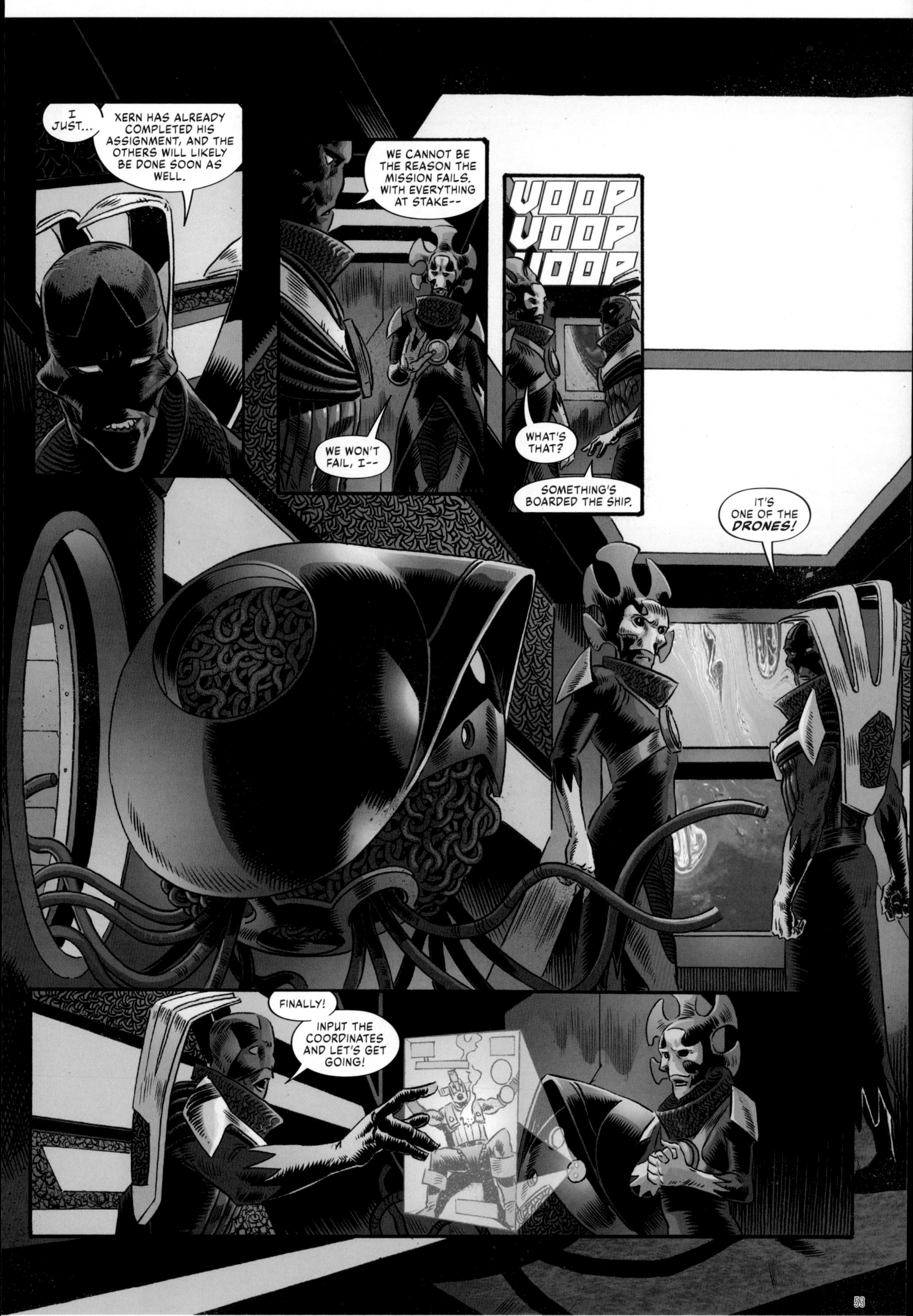

I JUST...
XERN HAS ALREADY COMPLETED HIS ASSIGNMENT, AND THE OTHERS WILL LIKELY BE DONE SOON AS WELL.
WE CANNOT BE THE REASON THE MISSION FAILS. WITH EVERYTHING AT STAKE--
WE WON'T FAIL, I--
VOOP VOOP VOOP
WHAT'S THAT?
SOMETHING'S BOARDED THE SHIP.
IT'S ONE OF THE DRONES!
FINALLY!
INPUT THE COORDINATES AND LET'S GET GOING!

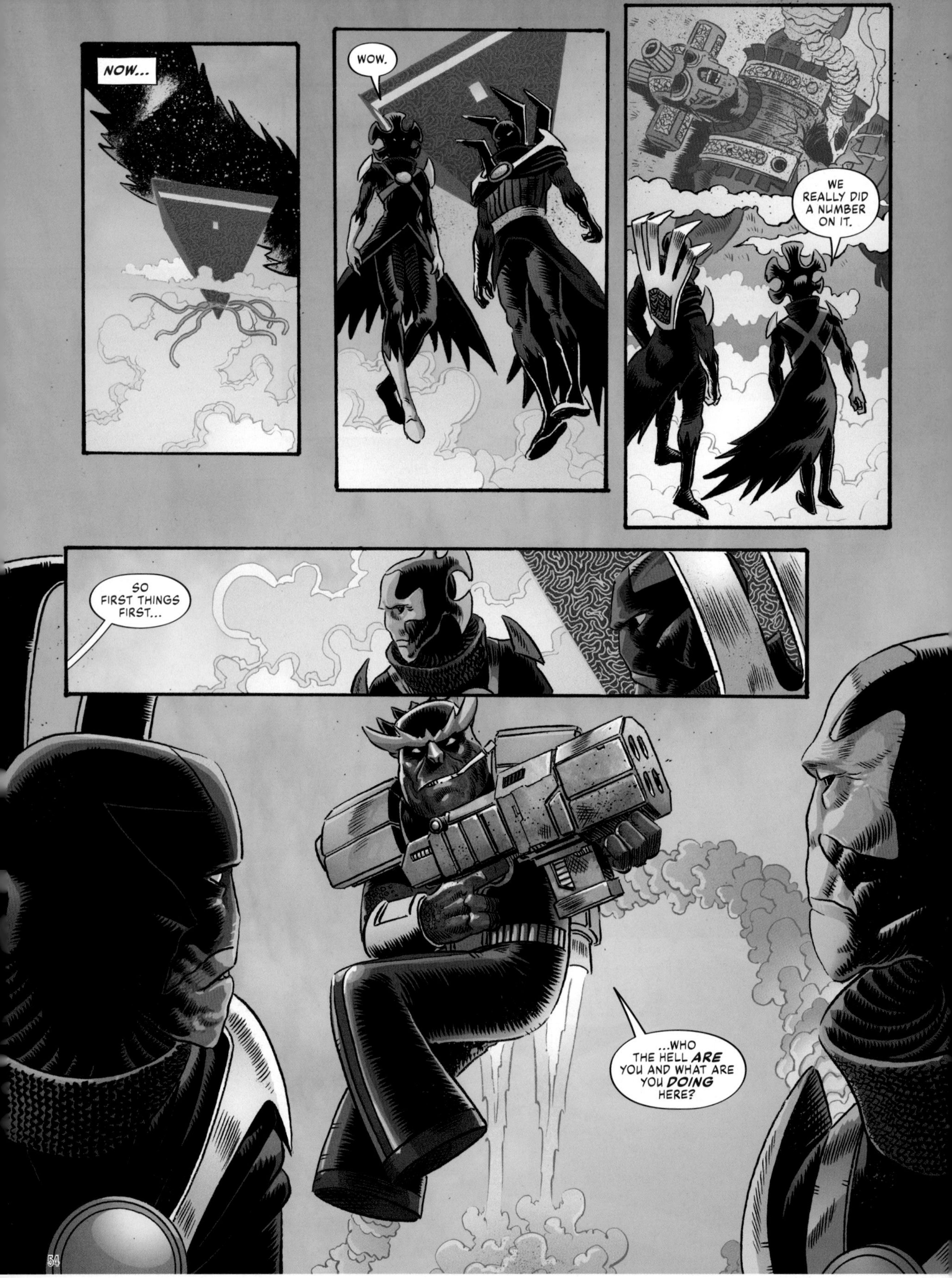
NOW...
WOW.
WE REALLY DID A NUMBER ON IT.
SO FIRST THINGS FIRST...
...WHO THE HELL ARE YOU AND WHAT ARE YOU DOING HERE?

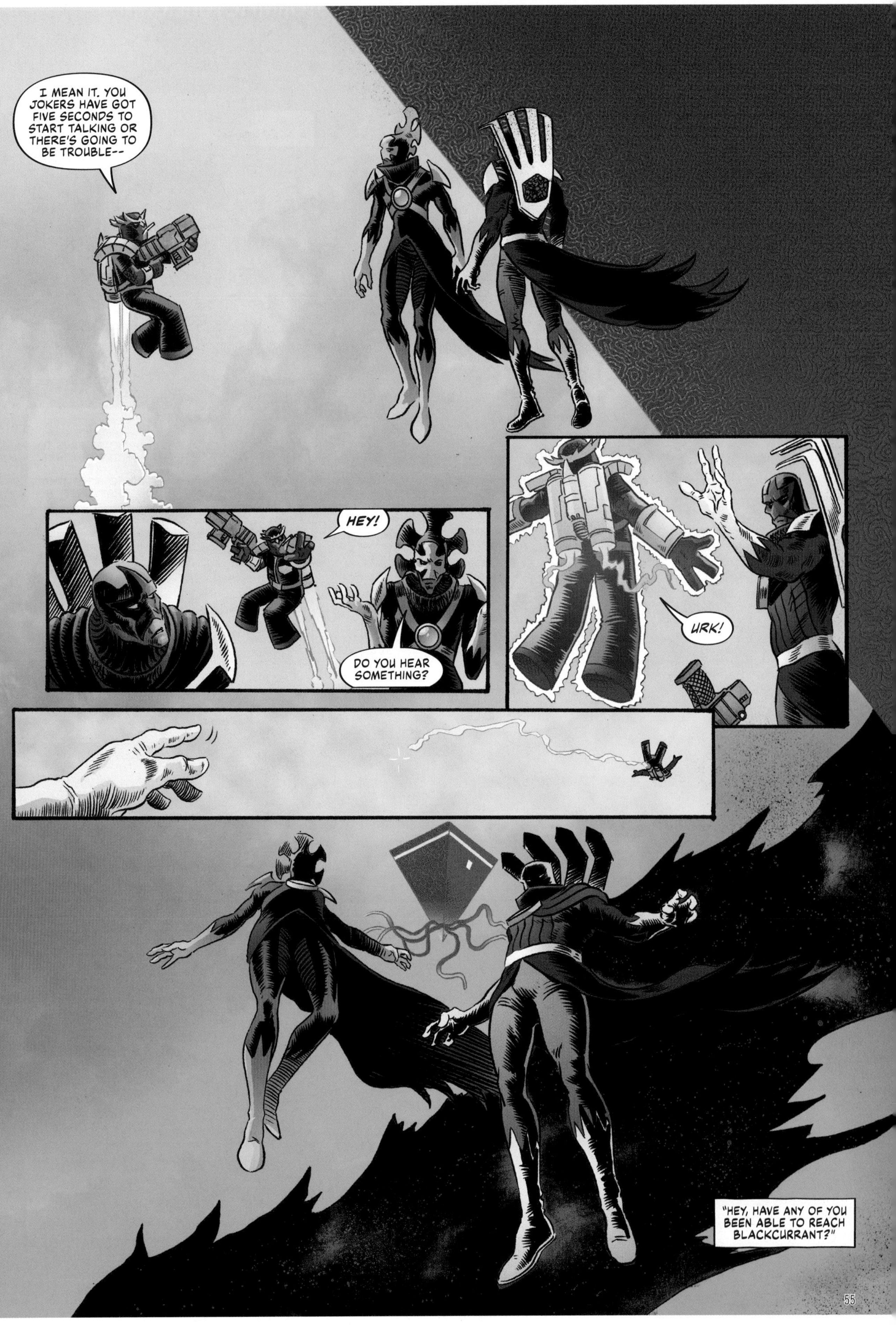
I MEAN IT. YOU JOKERS HAVE GOT FIVE SECONDS TO START TALKING OR THERE'S GOING TO BE TROUBLE--
HEY!
DO YOU HEAR SOMETHING?
URK!
"HEY, HAVE ANY OF YOU BEEN ABLE TO REACH BLACKCURRANT?"

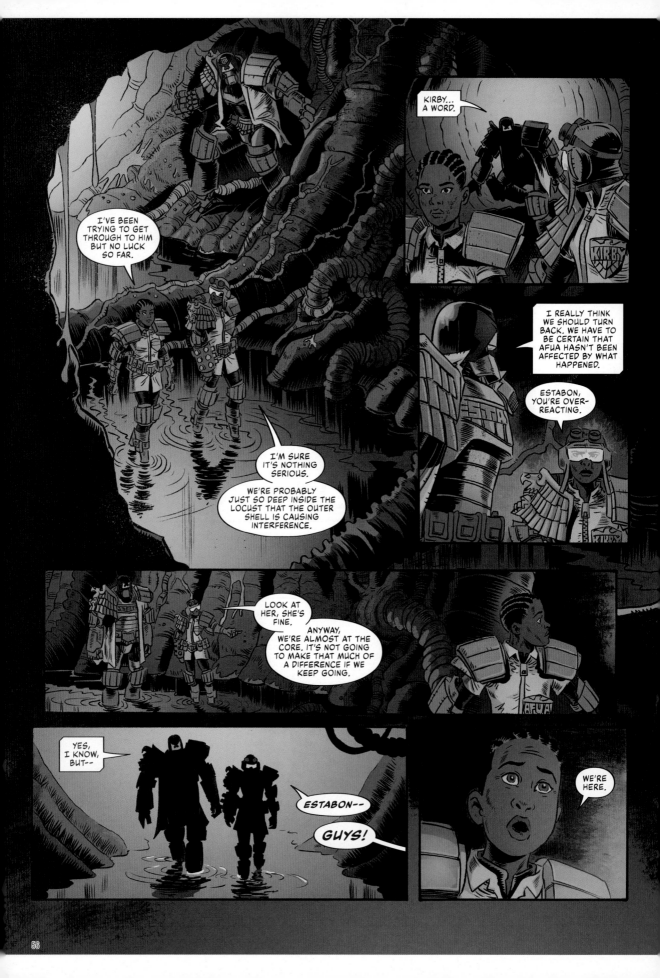

I'VE BEEN TRYING TO GET THROUGH TO HIM BUT NO LUCK SO FAR.

KIRBY... A WORD.

I'M SURE IT'S NOTHING SERIOUS.

WE'RE PROBABLY JUST SO DEEP INSIDE THE LOCUST THAT THE OUTER SHELL IS CAUSING INTERFERENCE.

I REALLY THINK WE SHOULD TURN BACK. WE HAVE TO BE CERTAIN THAT AFUA HASN'T BEEN AFFECTED BY WHAT HAPPENED.

ESTABON, YOU'RE OVER-REACTING.

LOOK AT HER, SHE'S FINE.

ANYWAY, WE'RE ALMOST AT THE CORE. IT'S NOT GOING TO MAKE THAT MUCH OF A DIFFERENCE IF WE KEEP GOING.

YES, I KNOW, BUT--

ESTABON--

GUYS!

WE'RE HERE.

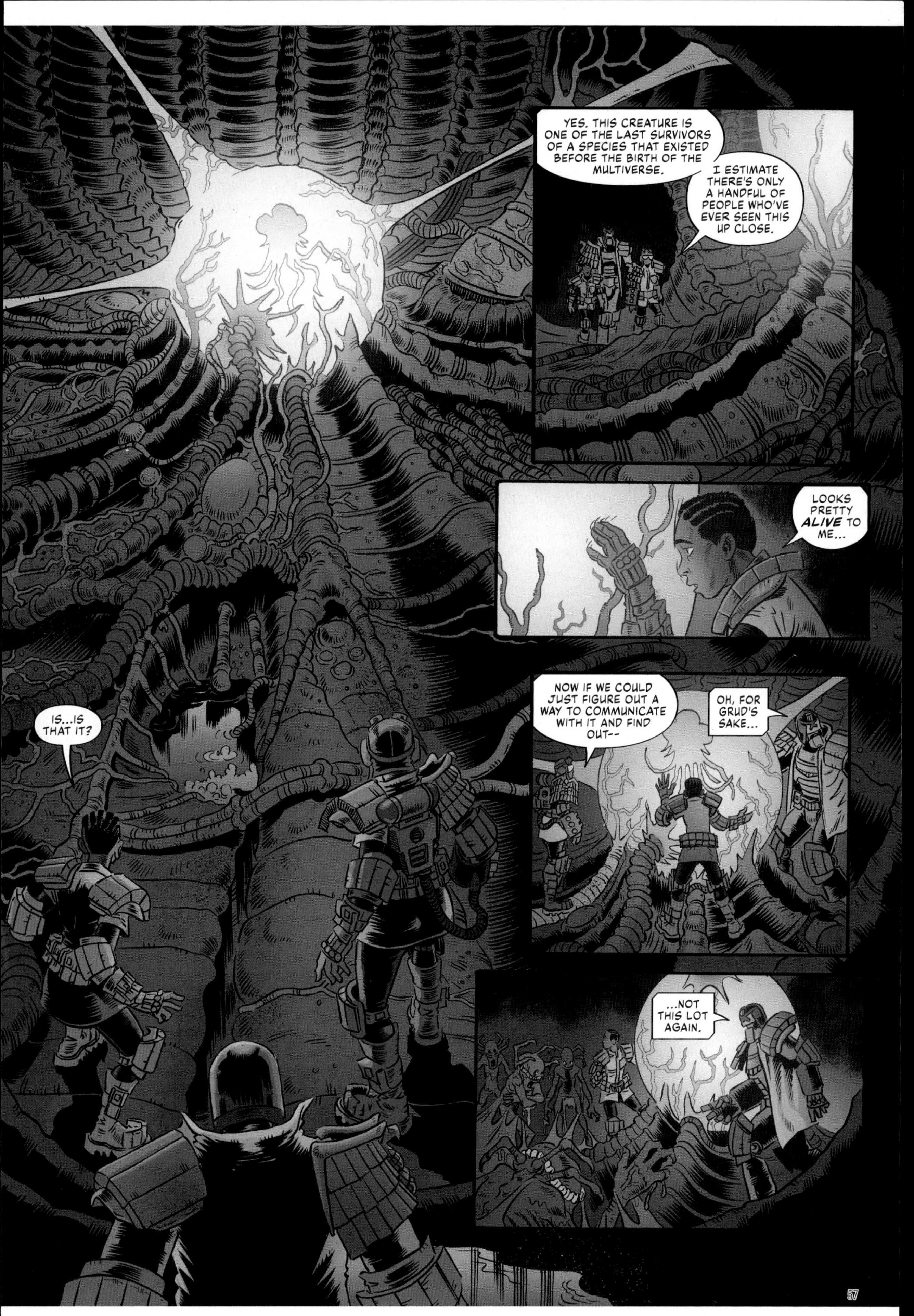
IS...IS THAT IT?
YES. THIS CREATURE IS ONE OF THE LAST SURVIVORS OF A SPECIES THAT EXISTED BEFORE THE BIRTH OF THE MULTIVERSE.
I ESTIMATE THERE'S ONLY A HANDFUL OF PEOPLE WHO'VE EVER SEEN THIS UP CLOSE.
LOOKS PRETTY ALIVE TO ME...
NOW IF WE COULD JUST FIGURE OUT A WAY TO COMMUNICATE WITH IT AND FIND OUT--
OH, FOR GRUD'S SAKE...
...NOT THIS LOT AGAIN.

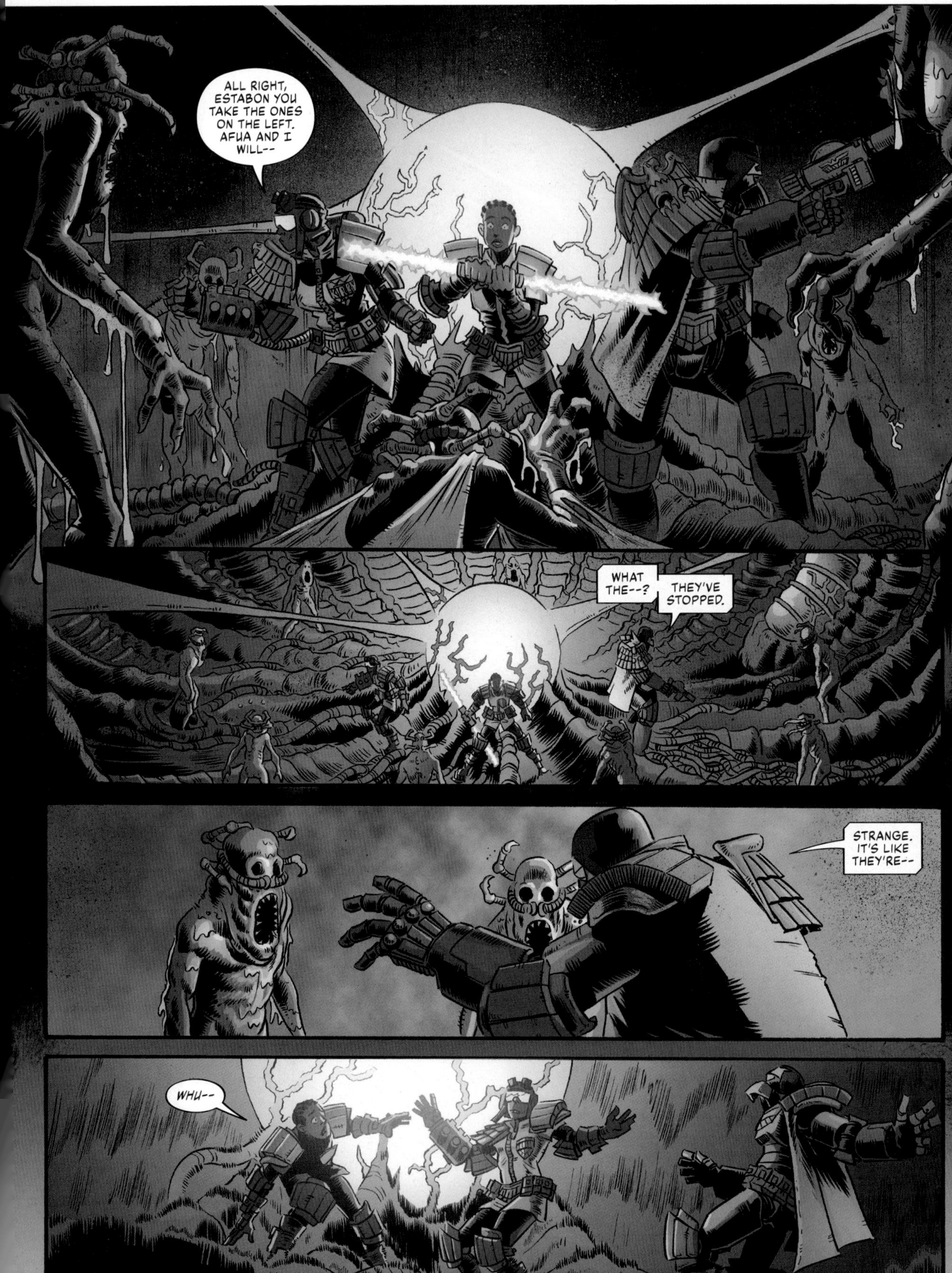
ALL RIGHT, ESTABON YOU TAKE THE ONES ON THE LEFT. AFUA AND I WILL--
WHAT THE--?
THEY'VE STOPPED.
STRANGE. IT'S LIKE THEY'RE--
WHU--

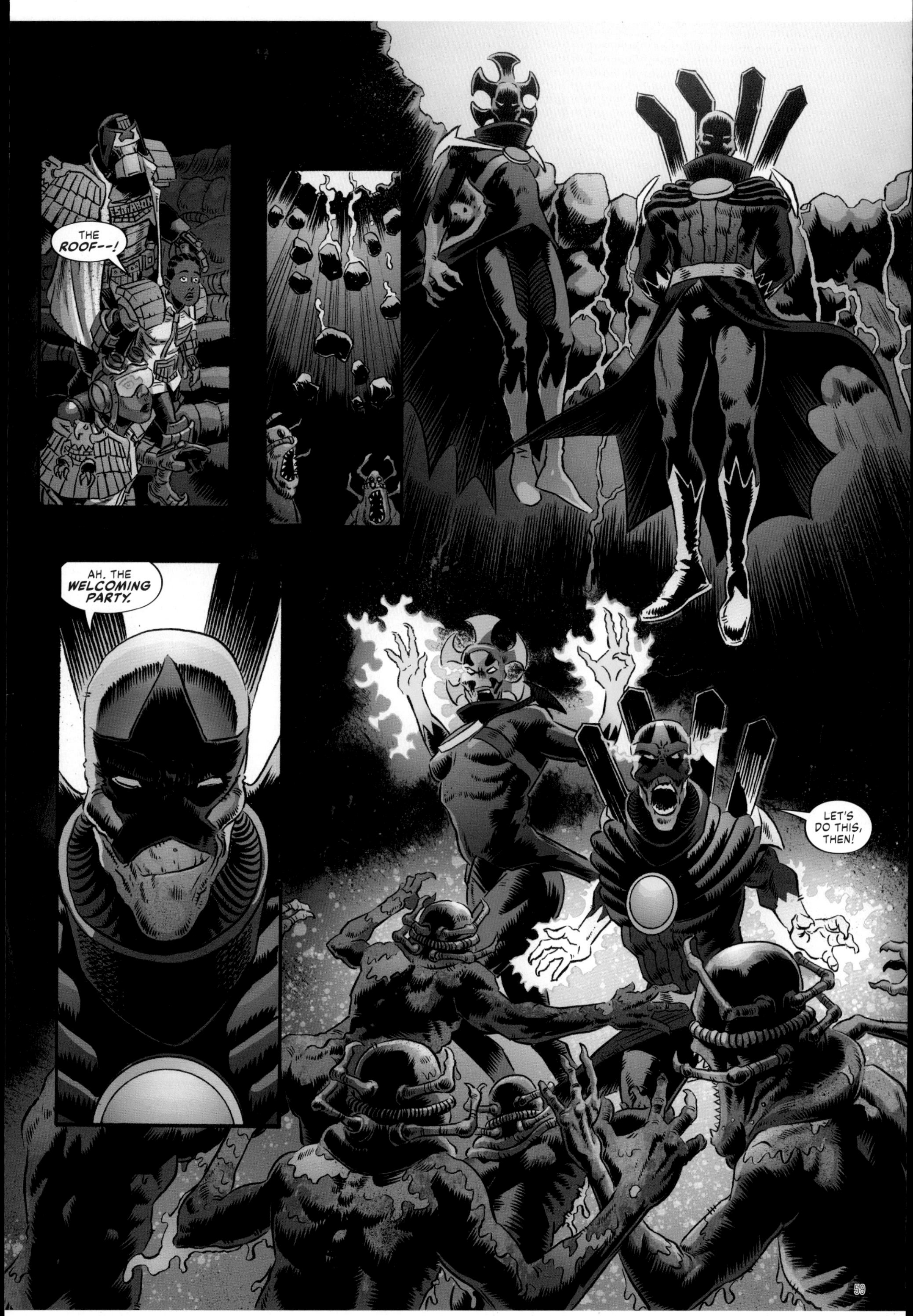
THE ROOF--!
AH. THE WELCOMING PARTY.
LET'S DO THIS, THEN!

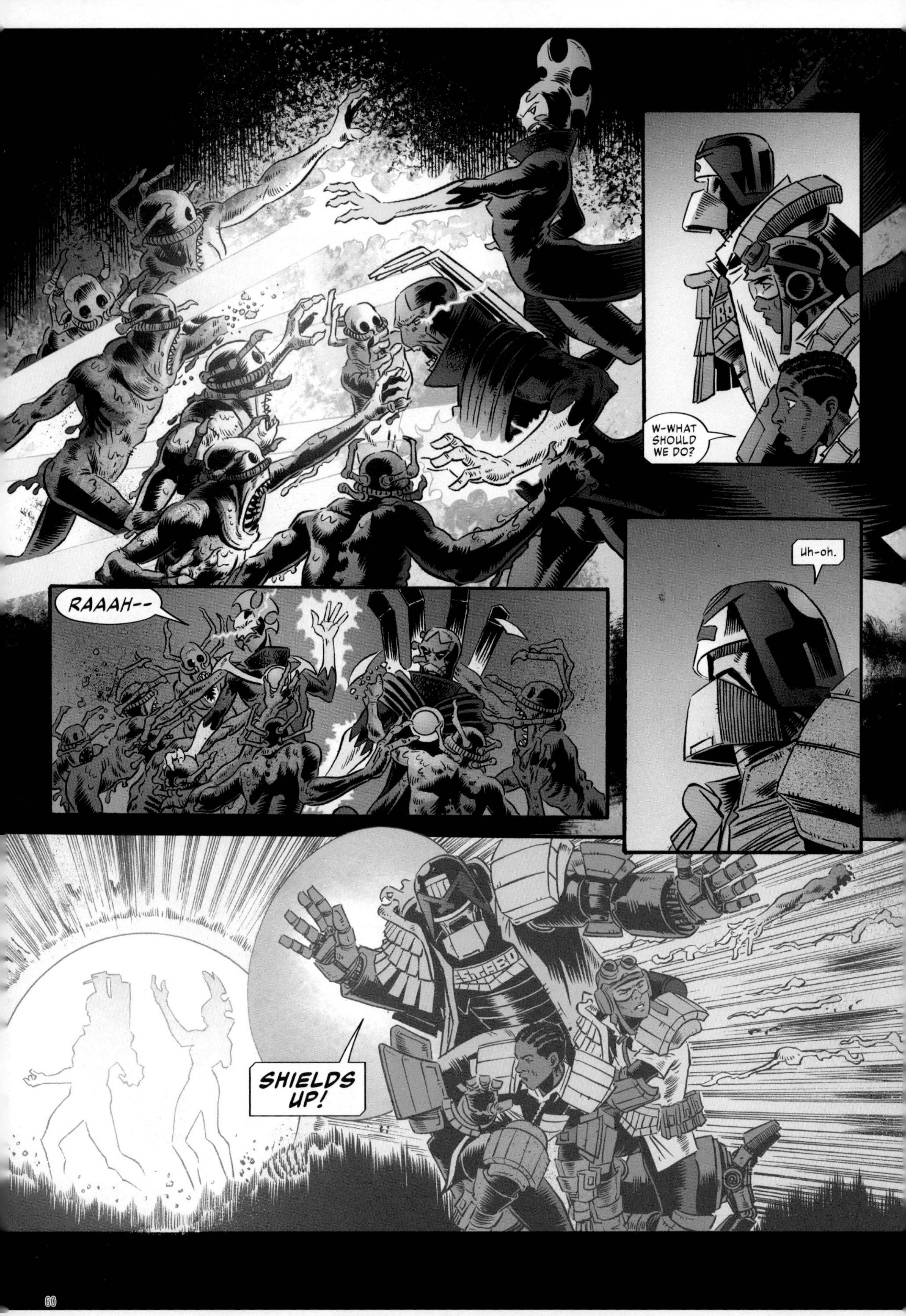
W-WHAT SHOULD WE DO?
Uh-oh.
RAAAH--
SHIELDS UP!

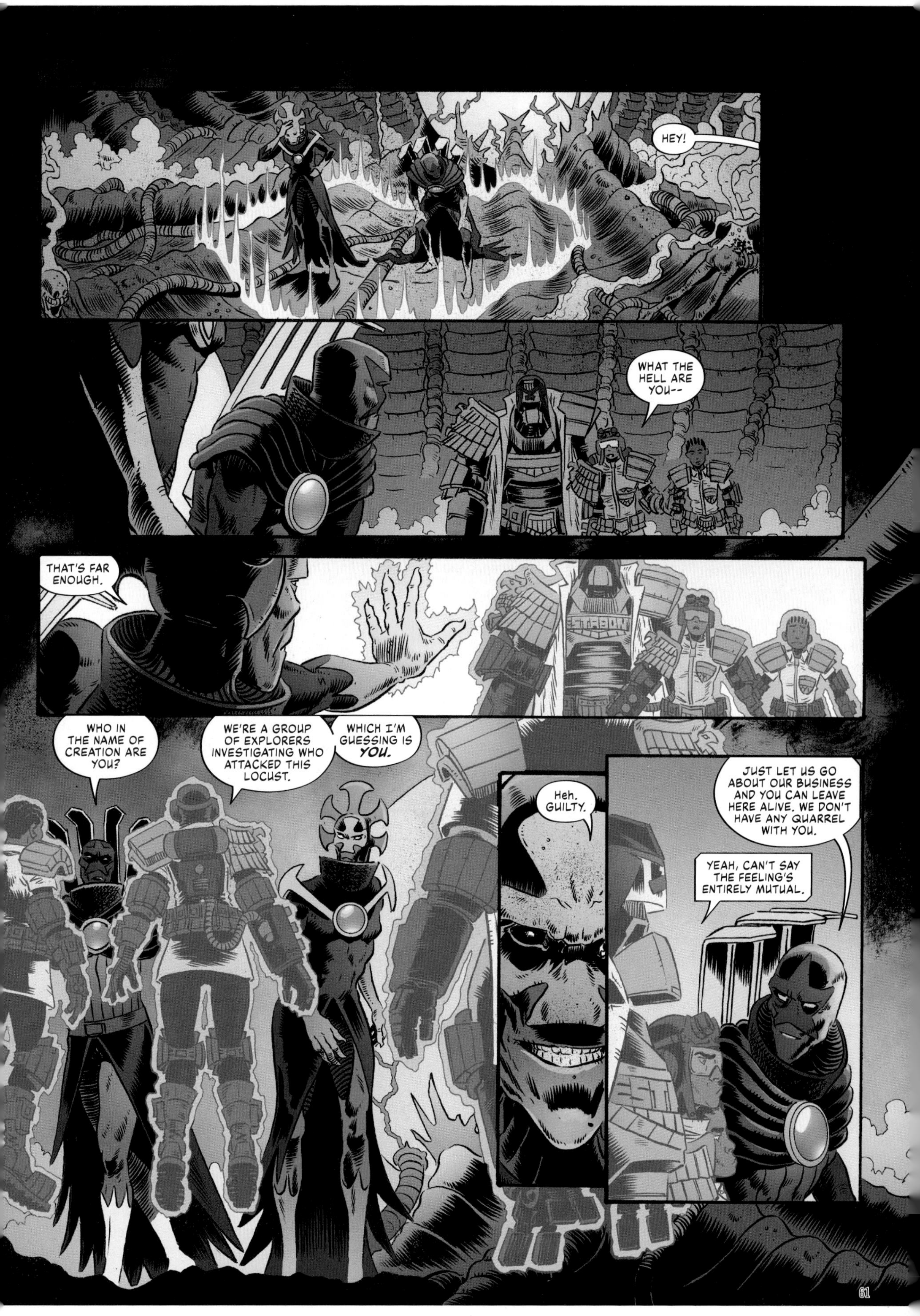
HEY!
WHAT THE HELL ARE YOU--
THAT'S FAR ENOUGH.
WHO IN THE NAME OF CREATION ARE YOU?
WE'RE A GROUP OF EXPLORERS INVESTIGATING WHO ATTACKED THIS LOCUST.
WHICH I'M GUESSING IS *YOU.*
Heh. GUILTY.
JUST LET US GO ABOUT OUR BUSINESS AND YOU CAN LEAVE HERE ALIVE. WE DON'T HAVE ANY QUARREL WITH YOU.
YEAH, CAN'T SAY THE FEELING'S ENTIRELY MUTUAL.

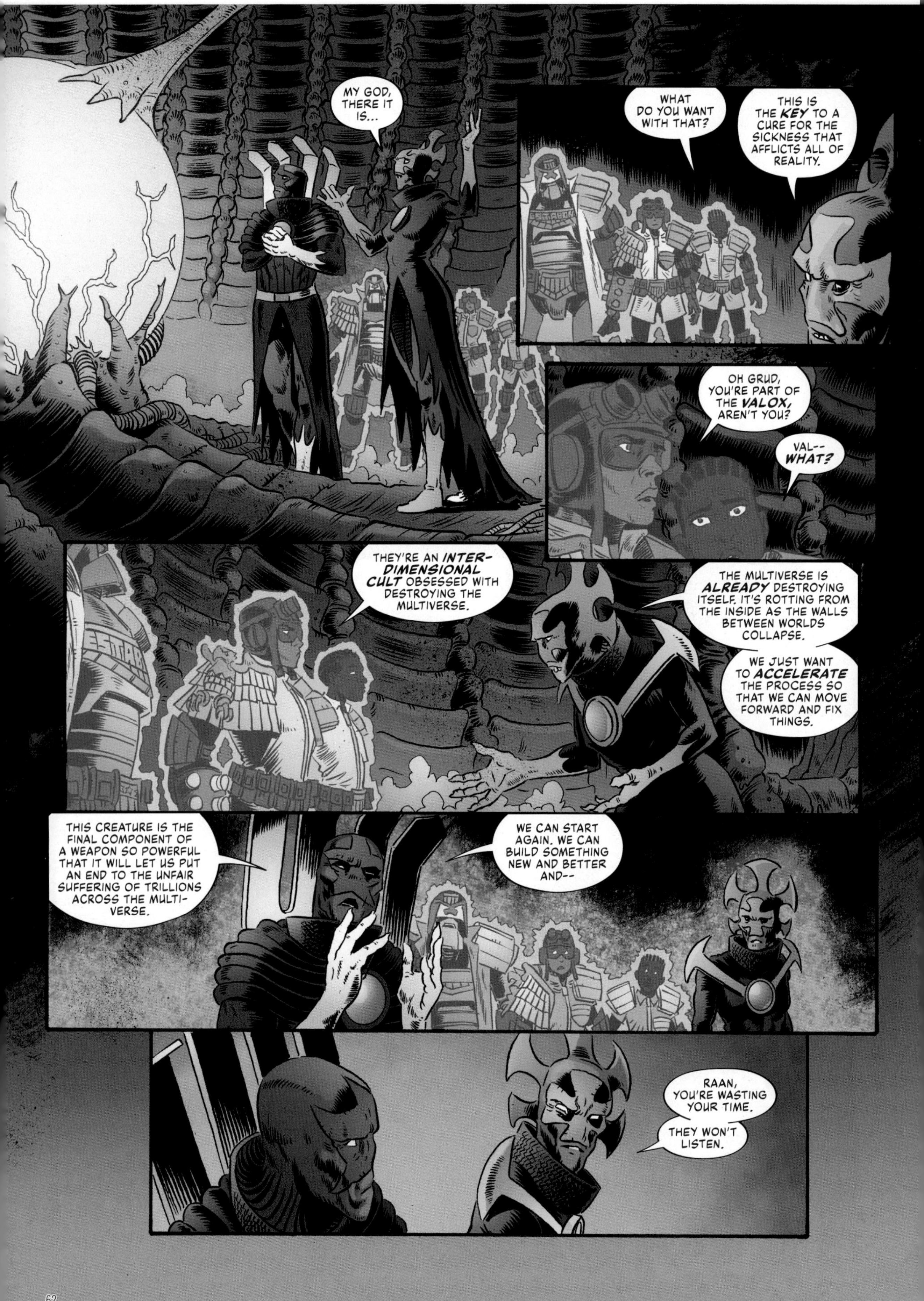
MY GOD, THERE IT IS...
WHAT DO YOU WANT WITH THAT?
THIS IS THE KEY TO A CURE FOR THE SICKNESS THAT AFFLICTS ALL OF REALITY.
OH GRUD, YOU'RE PART OF THE VALOX, AREN'T YOU?
VAL-- WHAT?
THEY'RE AN INTER-DIMENSIONAL CULT OBSESSED WITH DESTROYING THE MULTIVERSE.
THE MULTIVERSE IS ALREADY DESTROYING ITSELF. IT'S ROTTING FROM THE INSIDE AS THE WALLS BETWEEN WORLDS COLLAPSE.
WE JUST WANT TO ACCELERATE THE PROCESS SO THAT WE CAN MOVE FORWARD AND FIX THINGS.
THIS CREATURE IS THE FINAL COMPONENT OF A WEAPON SO POWERFUL THAT IT WILL LET US PUT AN END TO THE UNFAIR SUFFERING OF TRILLIONS ACROSS THE MULTI-VERSE.
WE CAN START AGAIN. WE CAN BUILD SOMETHING NEW AND BETTER AND--
RAAN, YOU'RE WASTING YOUR TIME.
THEY WON'T LISTEN.

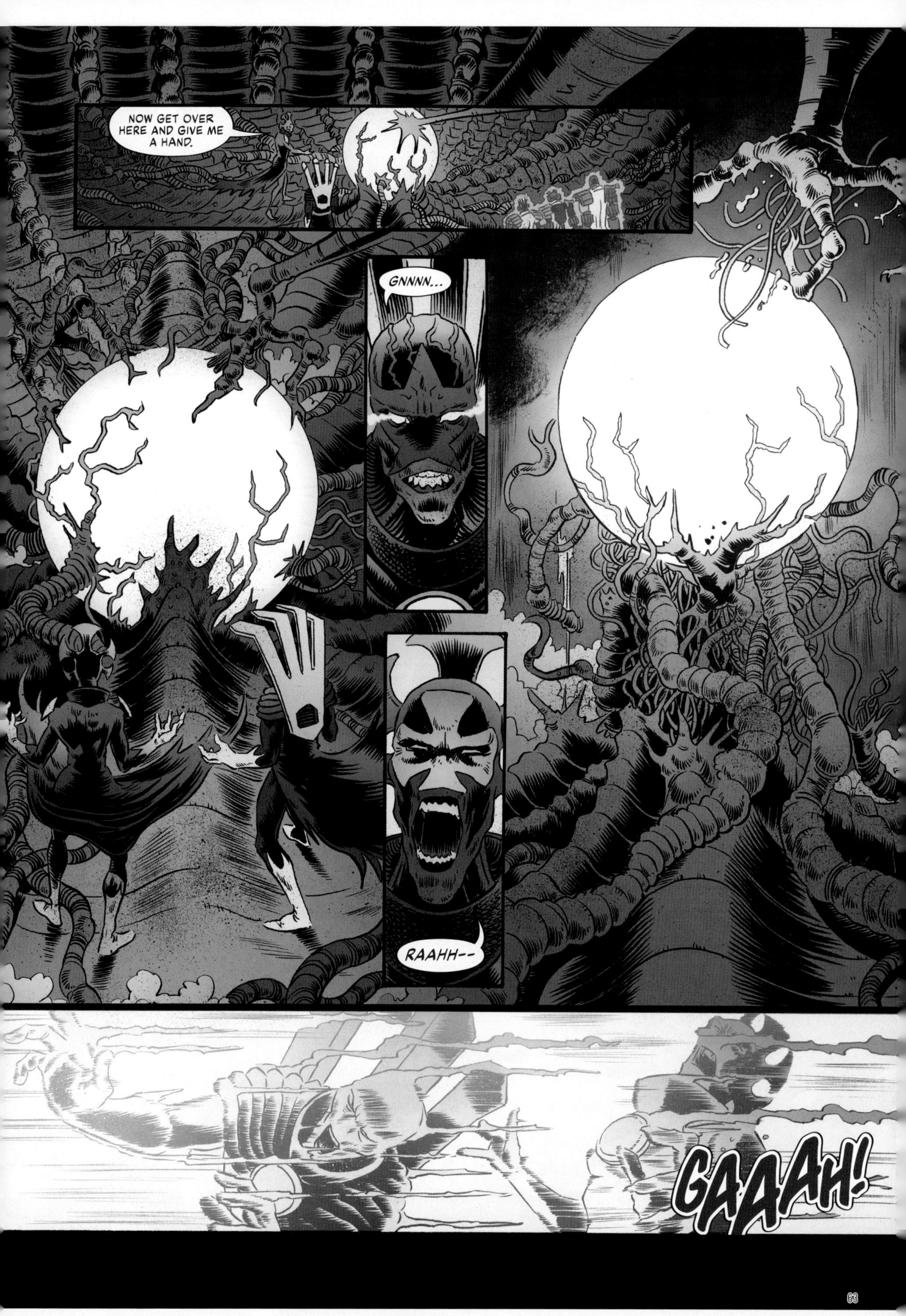
NOW GET OVER HERE AND GIVE ME A HAND.
GNNNN...
RAAHH--
GAAAH!

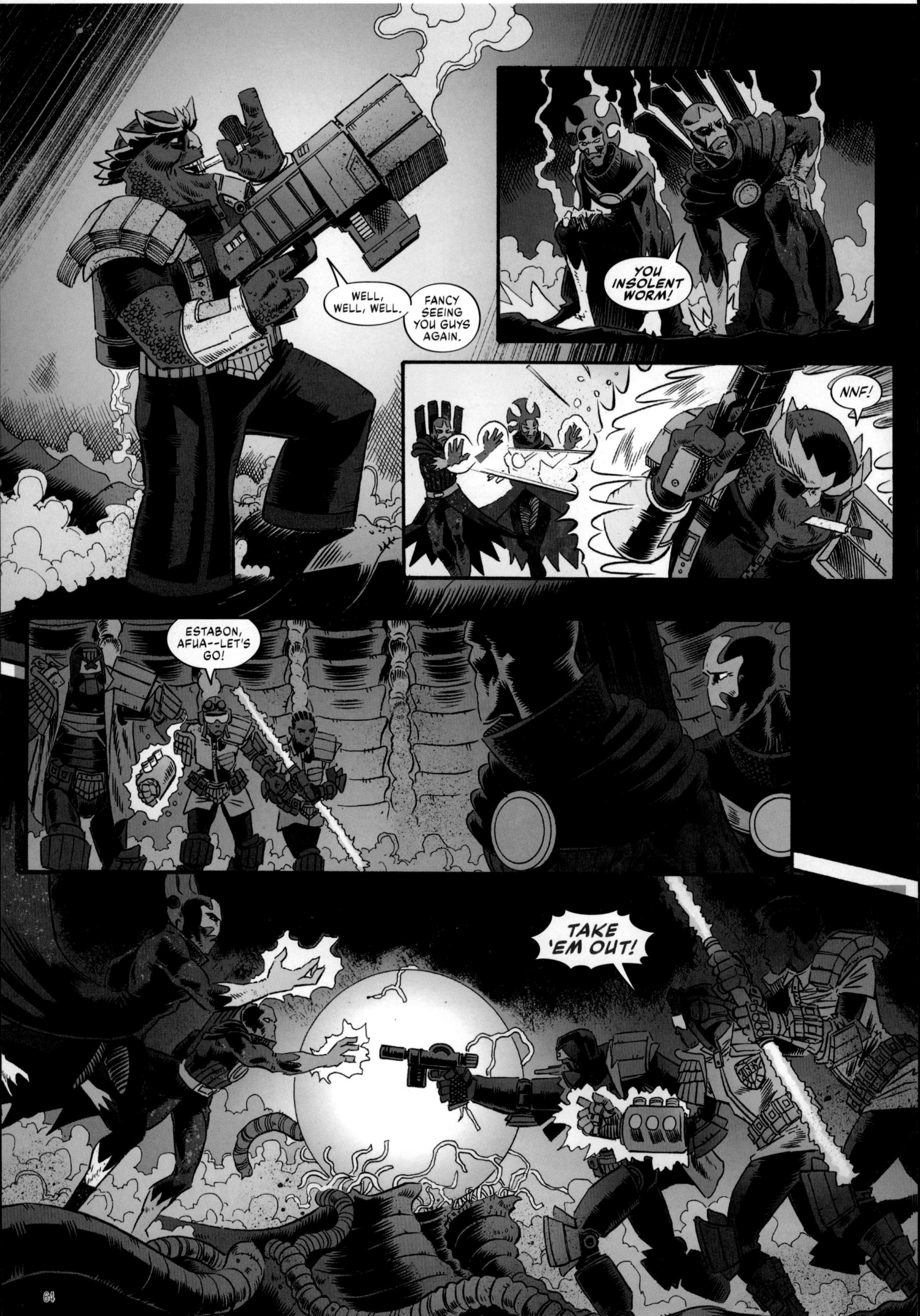
WELL, WELL, WELL.
FANCY SEEING YOU GUYS AGAIN.
YOU INSOLENT WORM!
NNF!
ESTABON, AFUA--LET'S GO!
TAKE 'EM OUT!

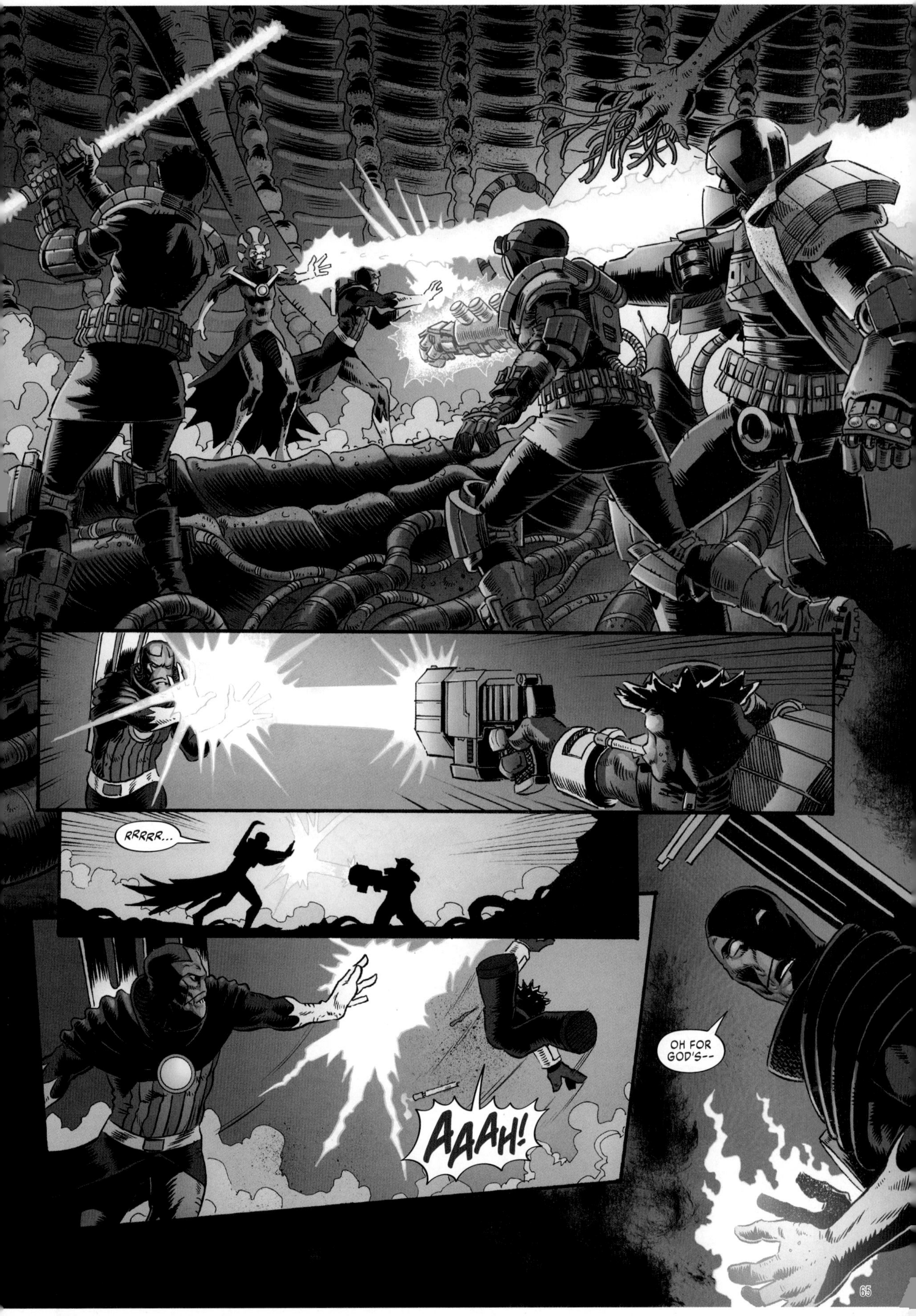
RRRRR...
OH FOR GOD'S--
AAAH!

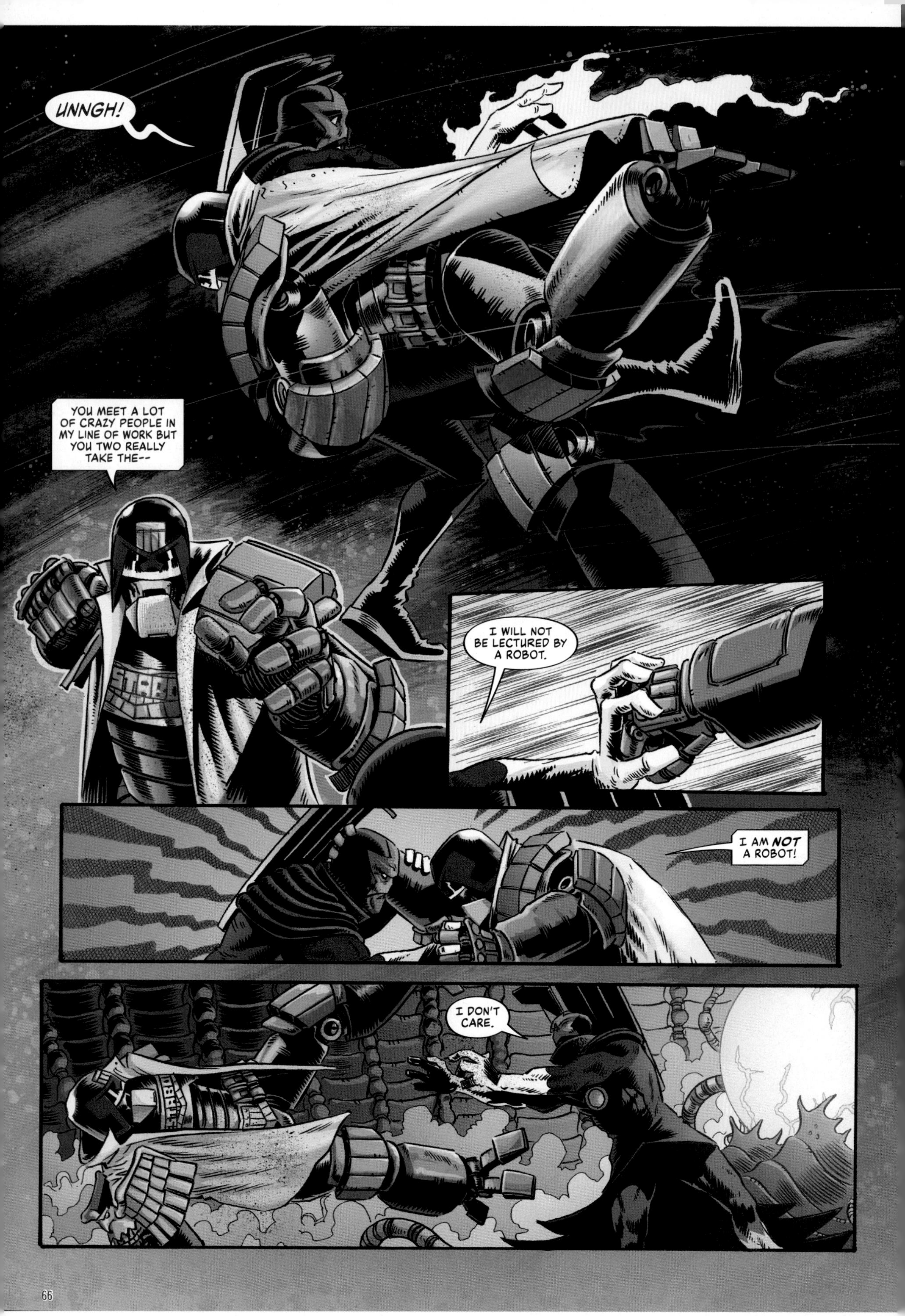
UNNGH!
YOU MEET A LOT OF CRAZY PEOPLE IN MY LINE OF WORK BUT YOU TWO REALLY TAKE THE--
I WILL NOT BE LECTURED BY A ROBOT.
I AM **NOT** A ROBOT!
I DON'T CARE.

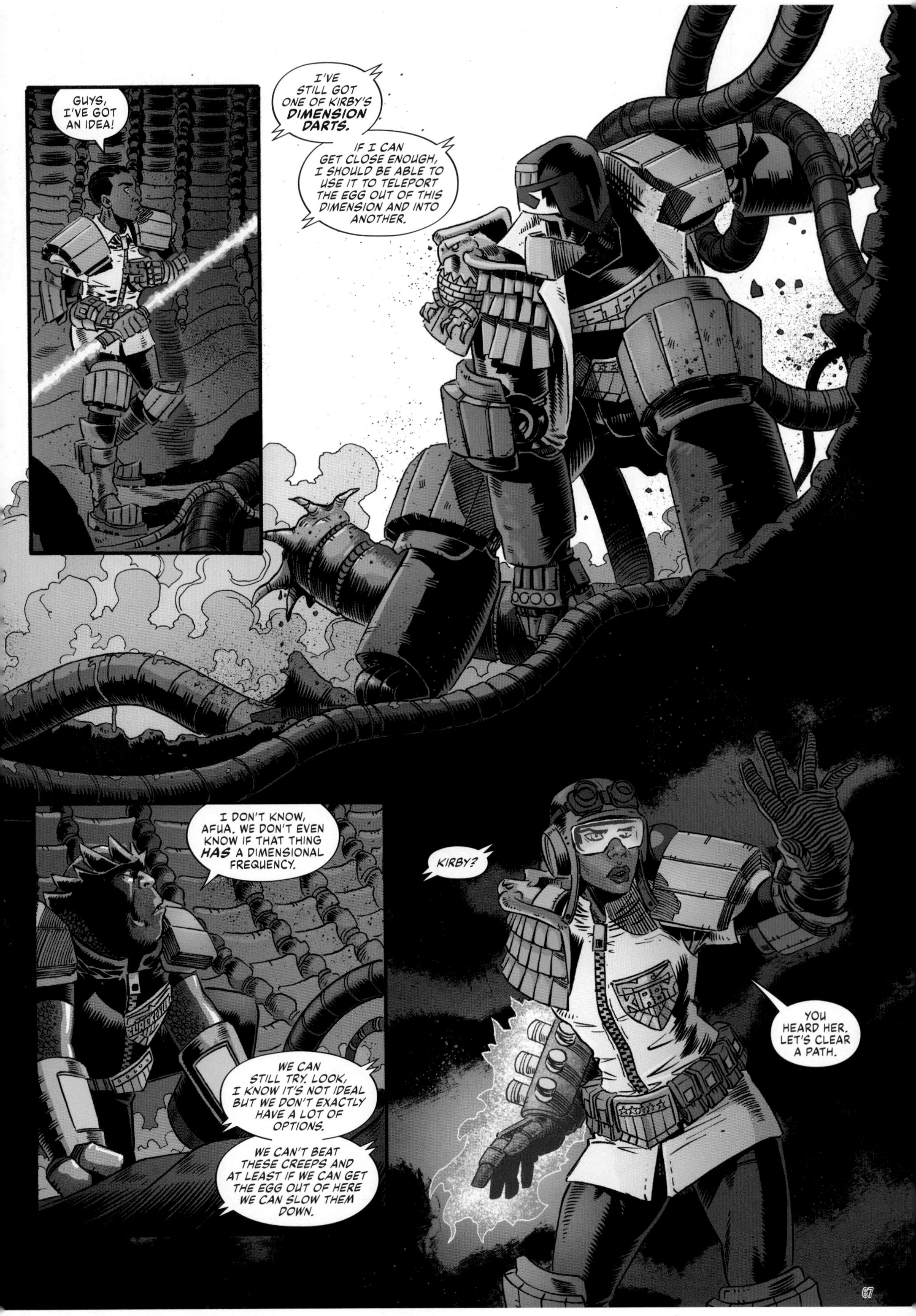
GUYS, I'VE GOT AN IDEA!
I'VE STILL GOT ONE OF KIRBY'S **DIMENSION DARTS.**
IF I CAN GET CLOSE ENOUGH, I SHOULD BE ABLE TO USE IT TO TELEPORT THE EGG OUT OF THIS DIMENSION AND INTO ANOTHER.
I DON'T KNOW, AFUA. WE DON'T EVEN KNOW IF THAT THING ***HAS*** A DIMENSIONAL FREQUENCY.
WE CAN STILL TRY. LOOK, I KNOW IT'S NOT IDEAL BUT WE DON'T EXACTLY HAVE A LOT OF OPTIONS.
WE CAN'T BEAT THESE CREEPS AND AT LEAST IF WE CAN GET THE EGG OUT OF HERE WE CAN SLOW THEM DOWN.
KIRBY?
YOU HEARD HER. LET'S CLEAR A PATH.

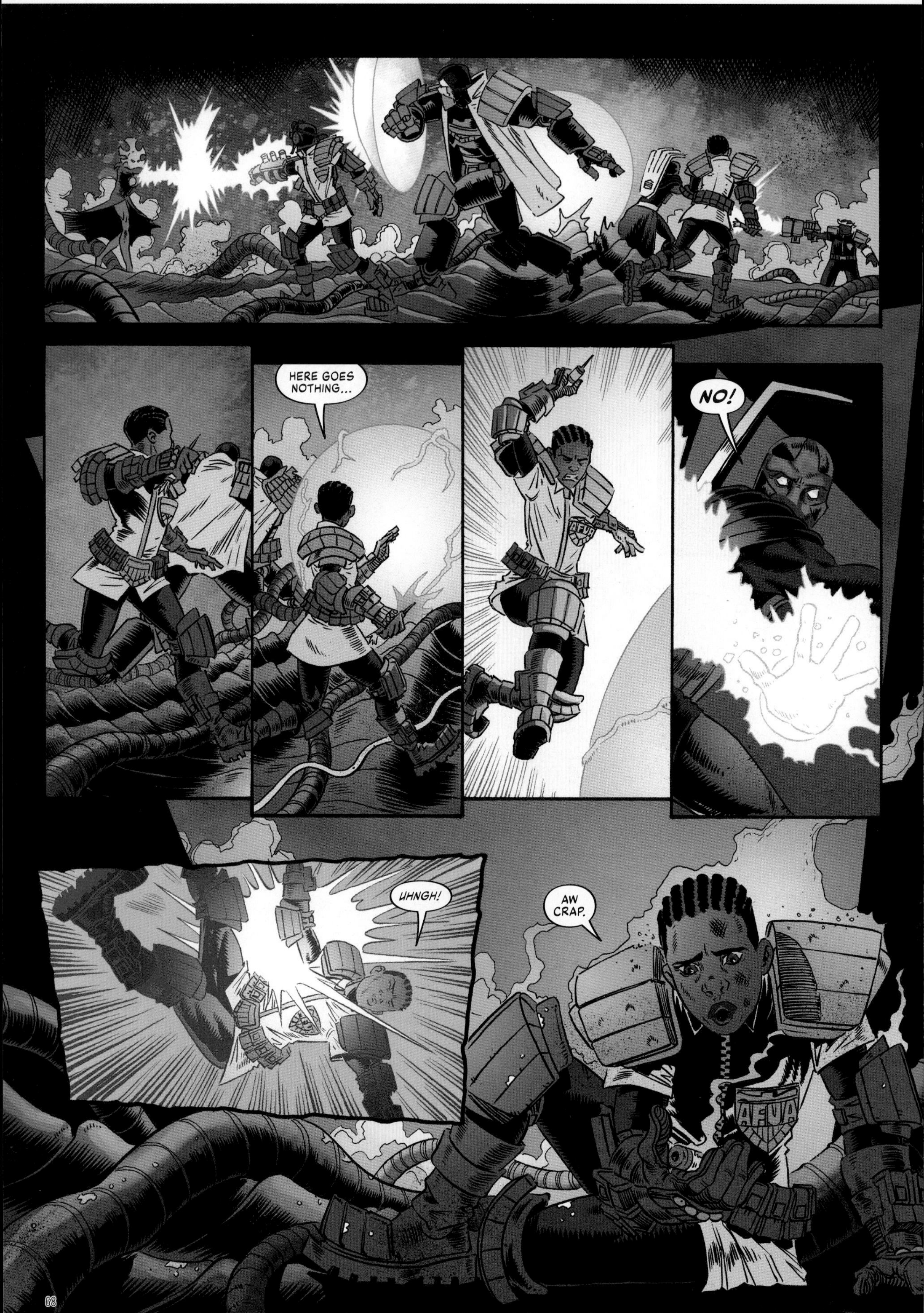
HERE GOES NOTHING...
NO!
UHNGH!
AW CRAP.
AFUA
AFUA

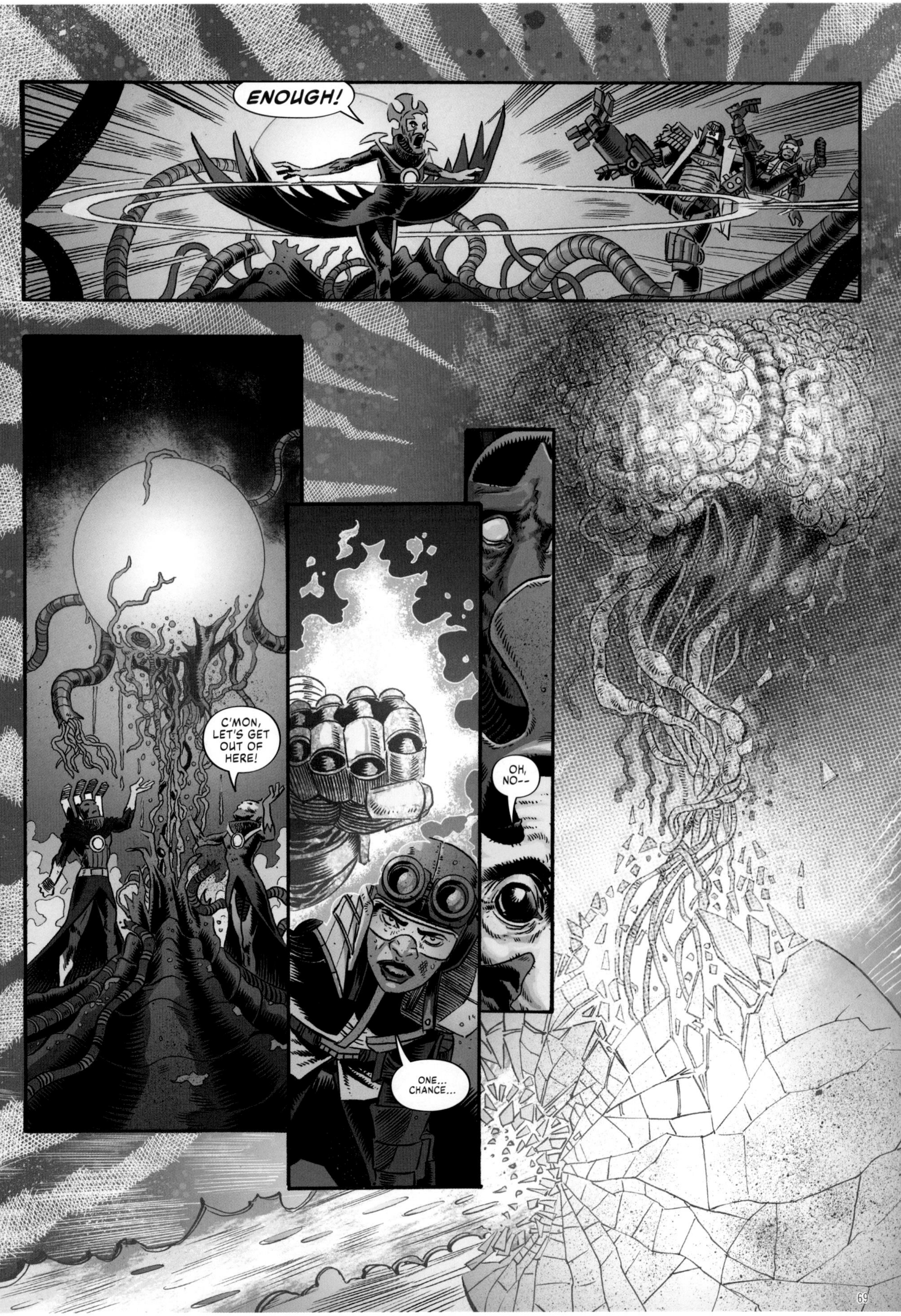
ENOUGH!
C'MON, LET'S GET OUT OF HERE!
ONE... CHANCE...
OH, NO--

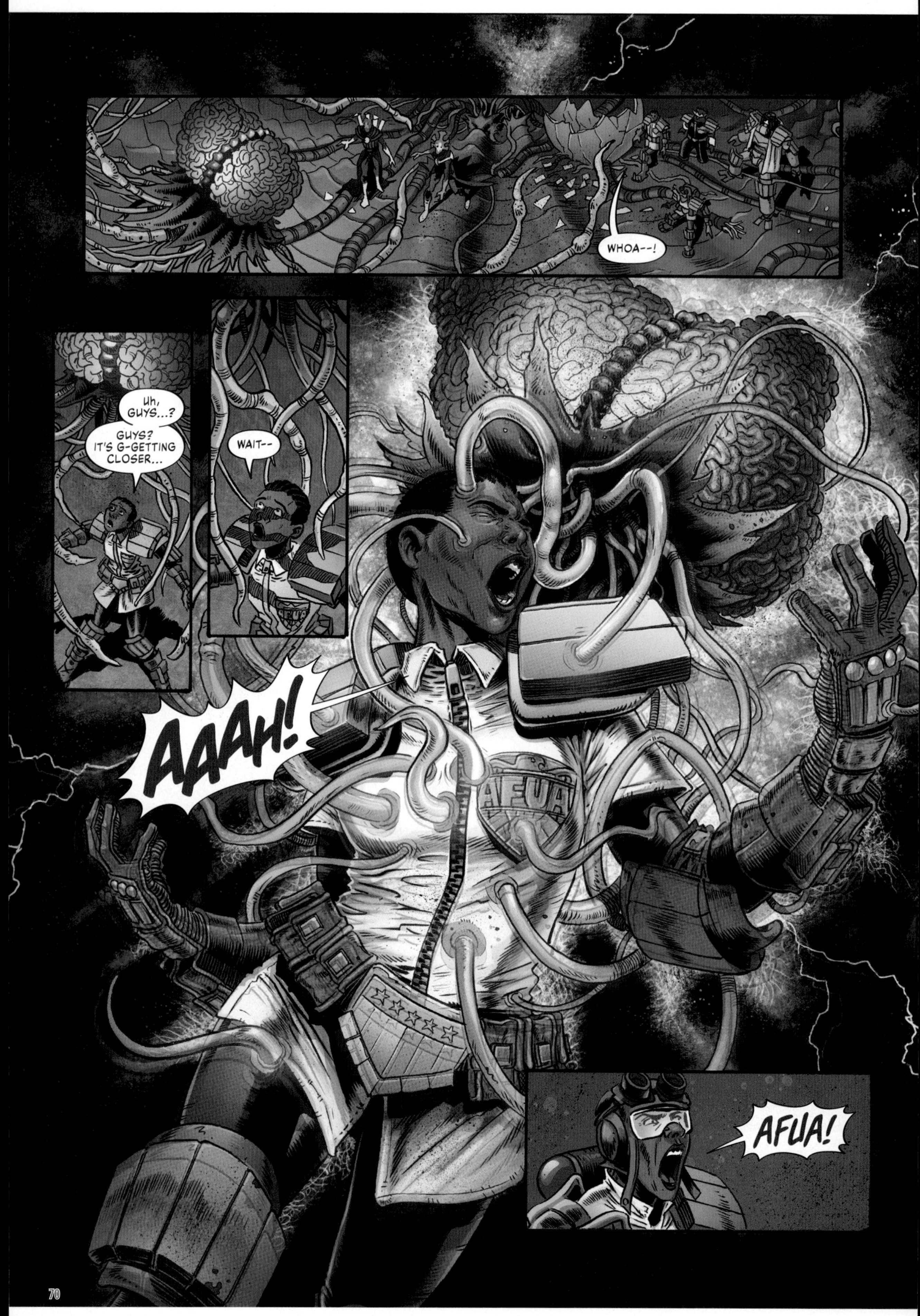

WHOA--!
UH, GUYS...?
GUYS? IT'S G-GETTING CLOSER...
WAIT--
AAAH!
AFUA!

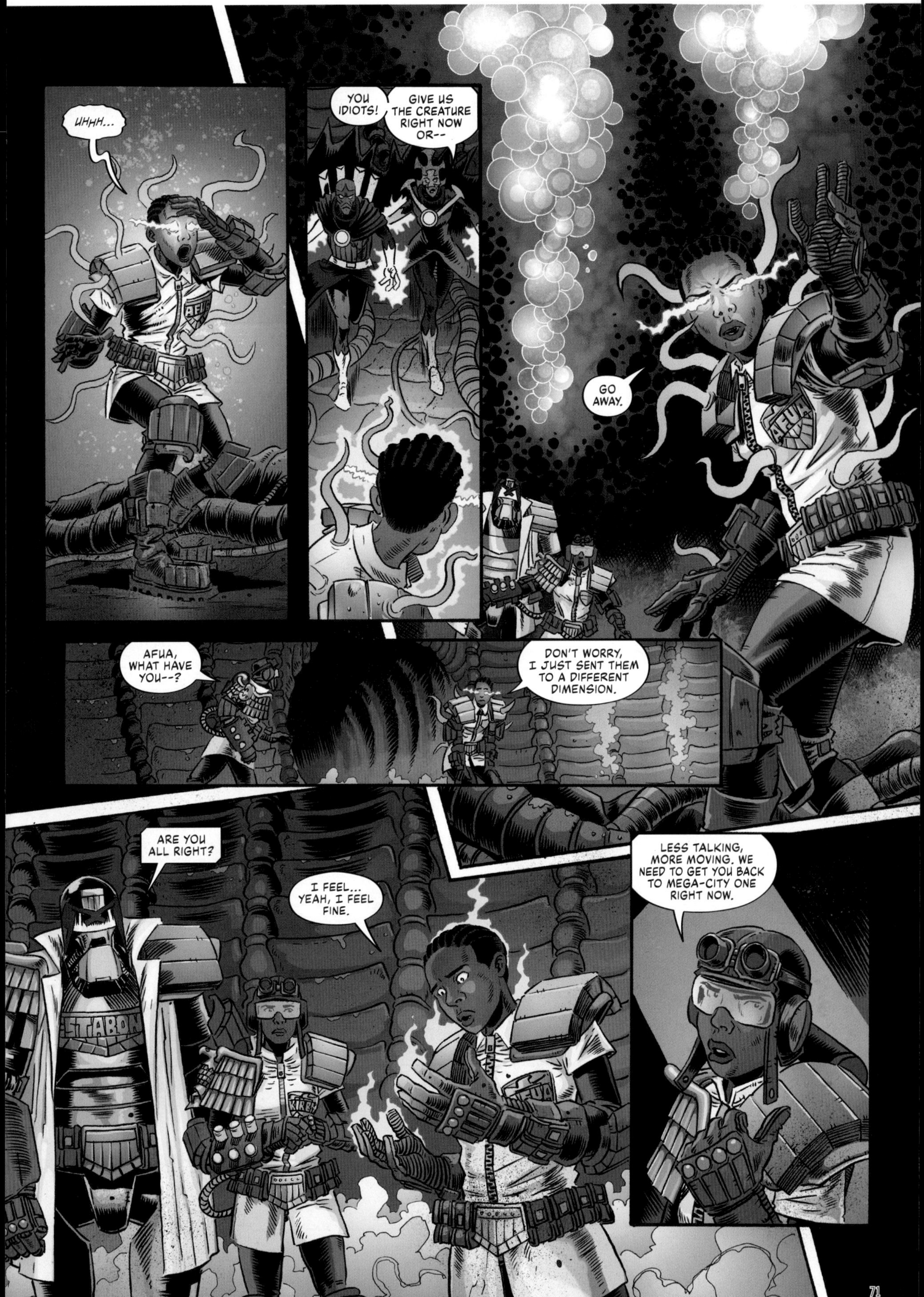
UHHH...
YOU IDIOTS!
GIVE US THE CREATURE RIGHT NOW OR--
GO AWAY.
AFUA, WHAT HAVE YOU--?
DON'T WORRY, I JUST SENT THEM TO A DIFFERENT DIMENSION.
ARE YOU ALL RIGHT?
I FEEL... YEAH, I FEEL FINE.
LESS TALKING, MORE MOVING. WE NEED TO GET YOU BACK TO MEGA-CITY ONE RIGHT NOW.

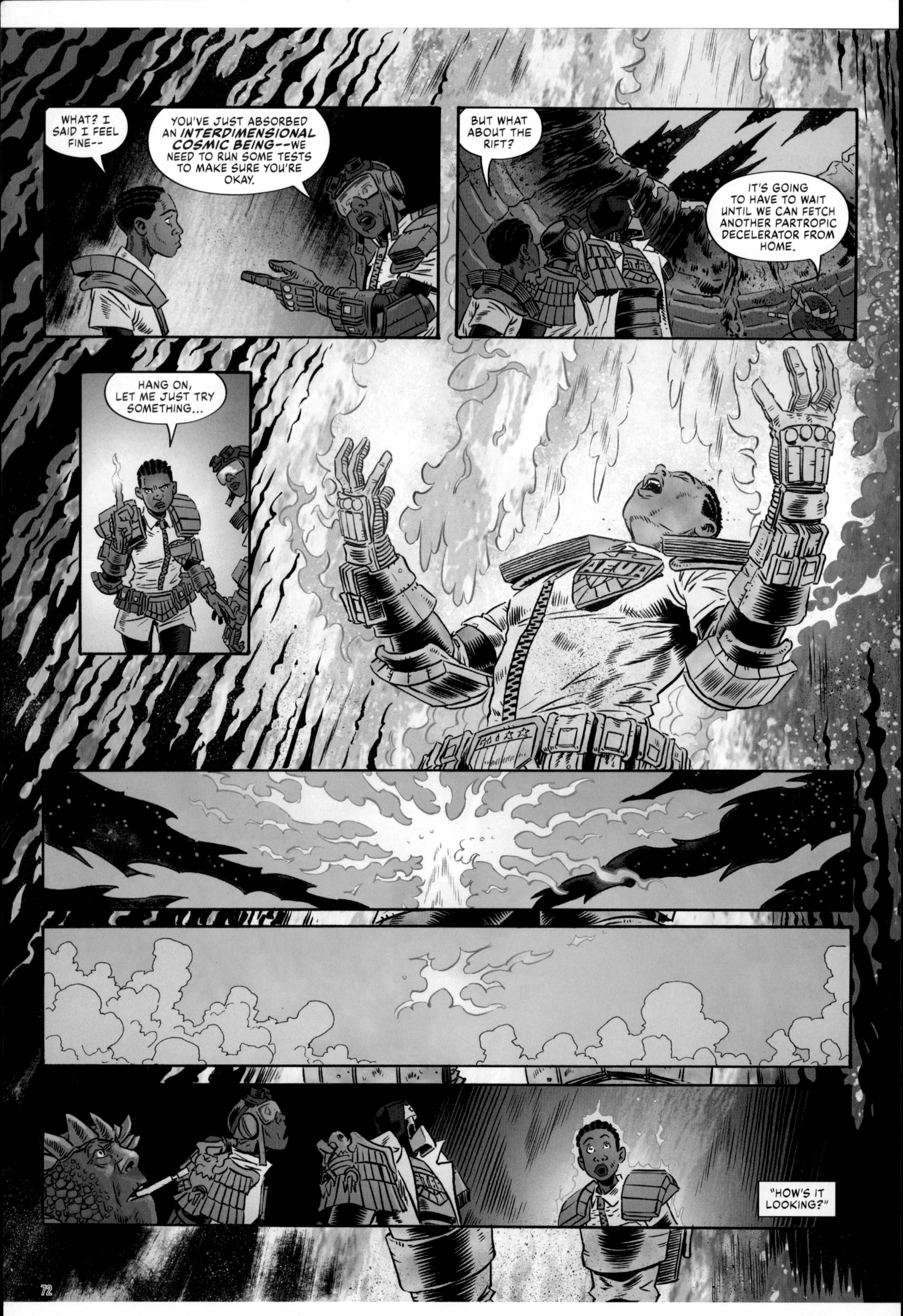
WHAT? I SAID I FEEL FINE--
YOU'VE JUST ABSORBED AN INTERDIMENSIONAL COSMIC BEING--WE NEED TO RUN SOME TESTS TO MAKE SURE YOU'RE OKAY.
BUT WHAT ABOUT THE RIFT?
IT'S GOING TO HAVE TO WAIT UNTIL WE CAN FETCH ANOTHER PARTROPIC DECELERATOR FROM HOME.
HANG ON, LET ME JUST TRY SOMETHING...
"HOW'S IT LOOKING?"

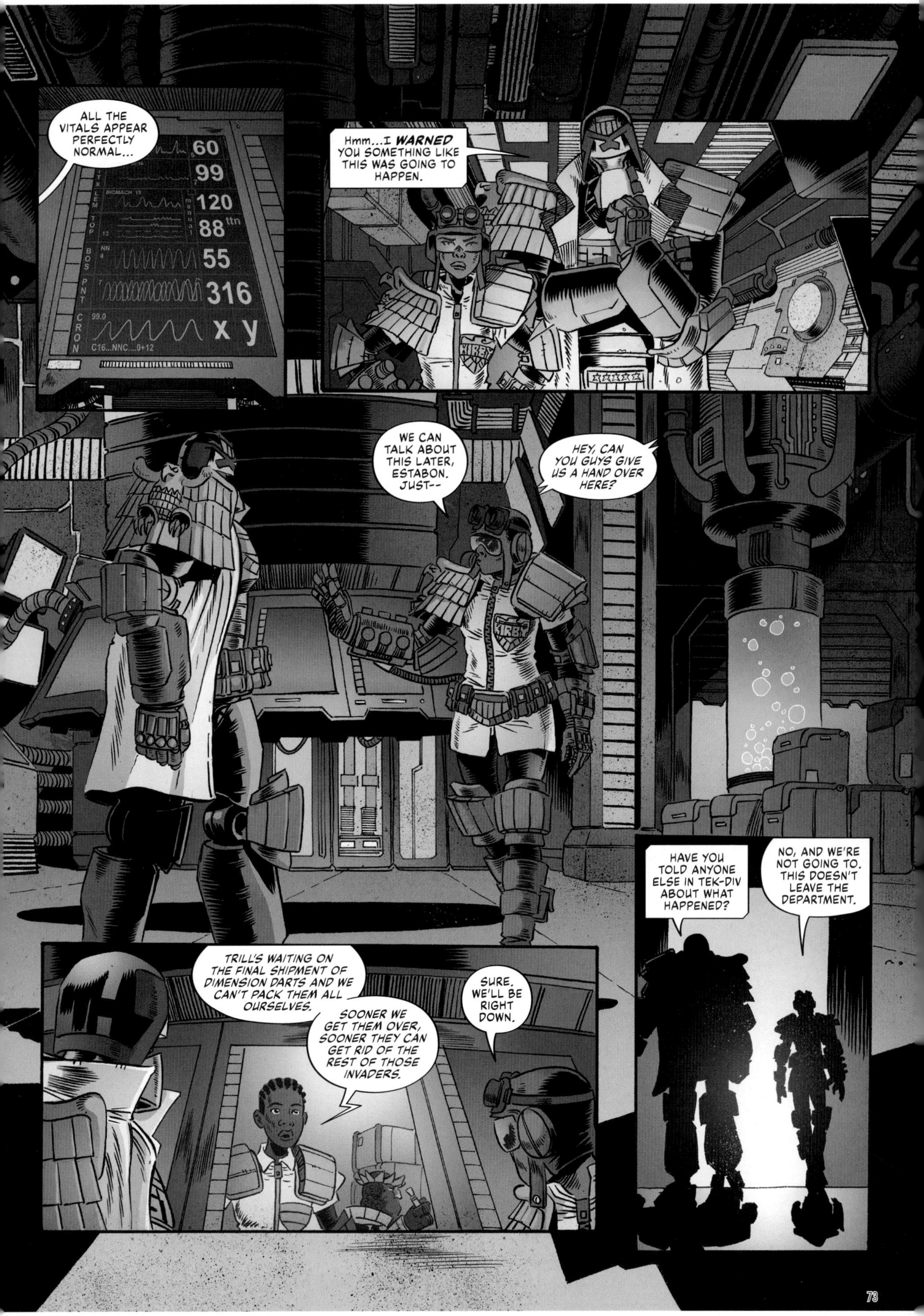
ALL THE VITALS APPEAR PERFECTLY NORMAL...
Hmm...I **WARNED** YOU SOMETHING LIKE THIS WAS GOING TO HAPPEN.
WE CAN TALK ABOUT THIS LATER, ESTABON. JUST--
HEY, CAN YOU GUYS GIVE US A HAND OVER HERE?
TRILL'S WAITING ON THE FINAL SHIPMENT OF DIMENSION DARTS AND WE CAN'T PACK THEM ALL OURSELVES.
SOONER WE GET THEM OVER, SOONER THEY CAN GET RID OF THE REST OF THOSE INVADERS.
SURE. WE'LL BE RIGHT DOWN.
HAVE YOU TOLD ANYONE ELSE IN TEK-DIV ABOUT WHAT HAPPENED?
NO, AND WE'RE NOT GOING TO. THIS DOESN'T LEAVE THE DEPARTMENT.

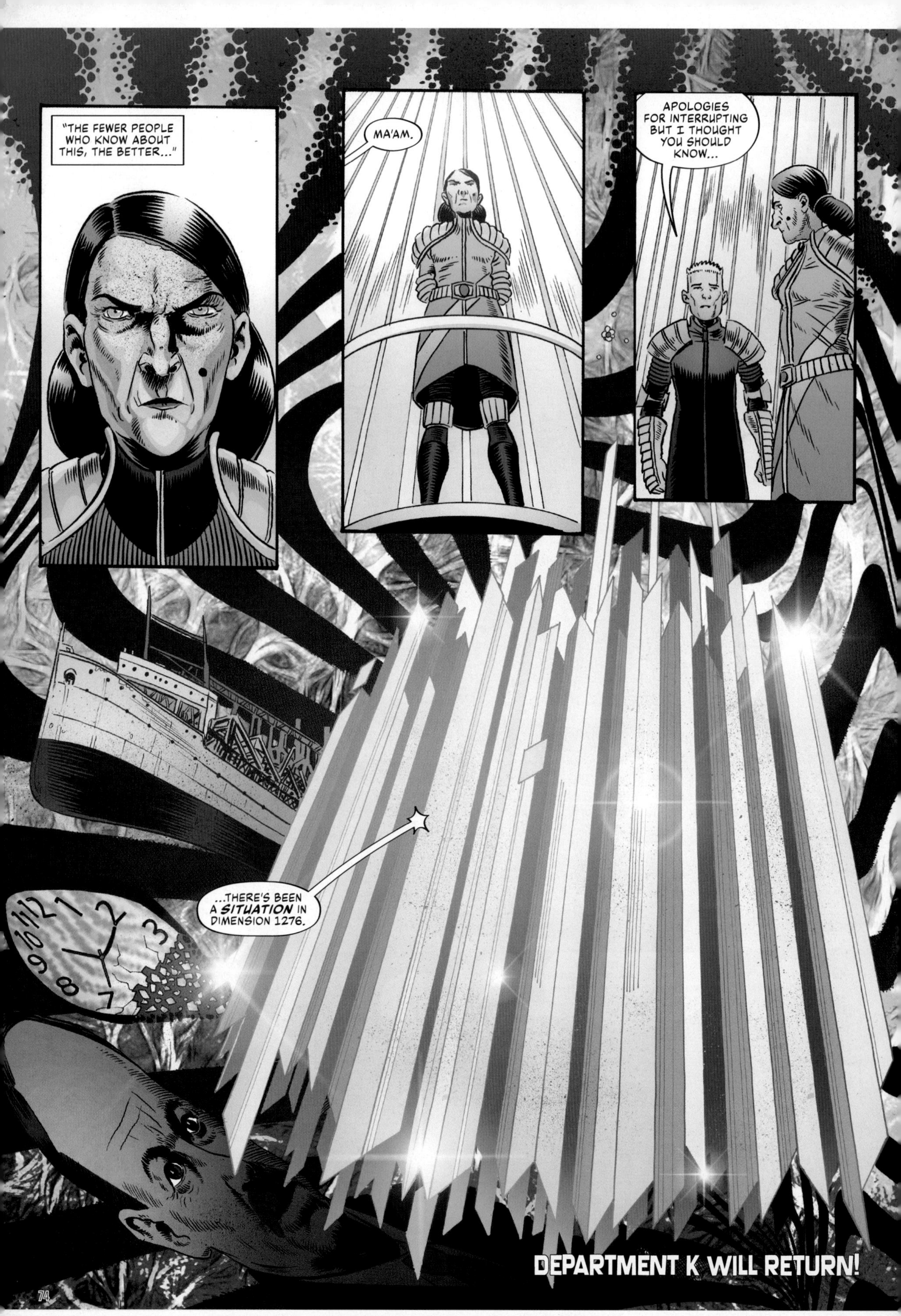
"THE FEWER PEOPLE WHO KNOW ABOUT THIS, THE BETTER..."
MA'AM.
APOLOGIES FOR INTERRUPTING BUT I THOUGHT YOU SHOULD KNOW...
...THERE'S BEEN A *SITUATION* IN DIMENSION 1276.
DEPARTMENT K WILL RETURN!

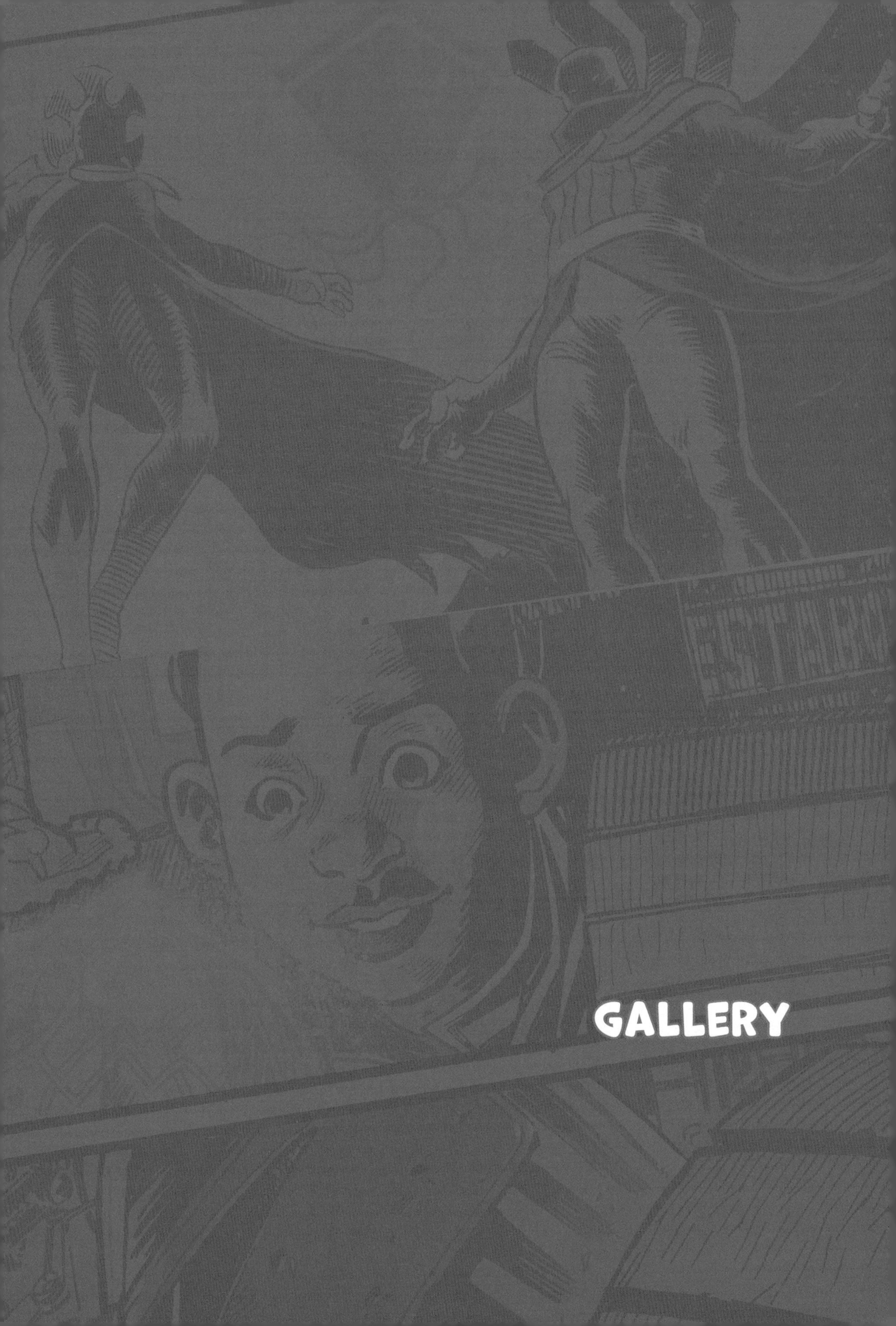

GALLERY

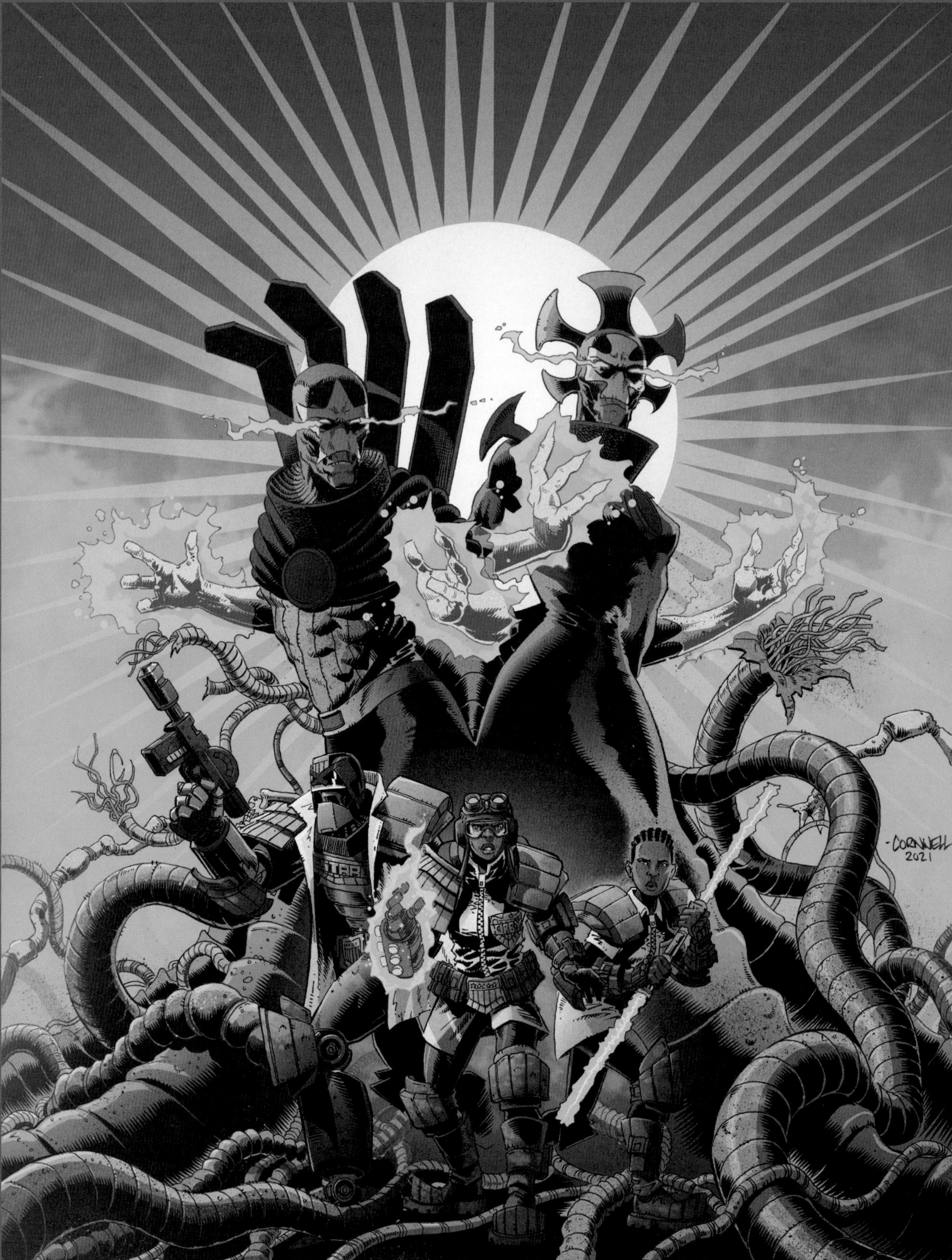
CORNWELL
2021

2000 AD Prog 2241: Cover by **Dan Cornwell**

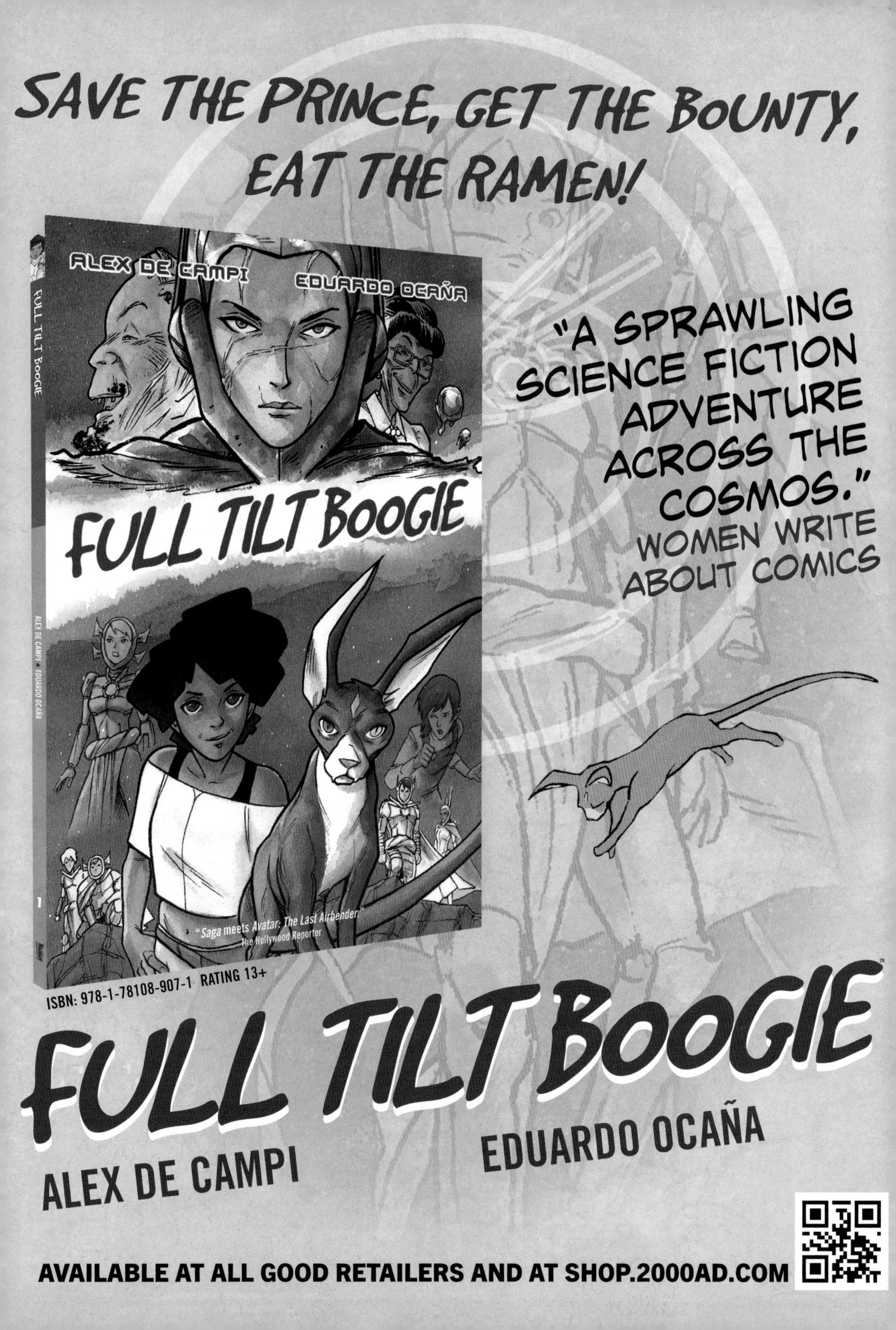
SAVE THE PRINCE, GET THE BOUNTY, EAT THE RAMEN!
ALEX DE CAMPI
EDUARDO OCAÑA
FULL TILT BOOGIE
"Saga meets Avatar: The Last Airbender."
The Hollywood Reporter
FULL TILT BOOGIE
ALEX DE CAMPI • EDUARDO OCAÑA
1
ISBN: 978-1-78108-907-1 RATING 13+
"A SPRAWLING SCIENCE FICTION ADVENTURE ACROSS THE COSMOS."
WOMEN WRITE ABOUT COMICS
FULL TILT BOOGIE™
ALEX DE CAMPI
EDUARDO OCAÑA
AVAILABLE AT ALL GOOD RETAILERS AND AT SHOP.2000AD.COM

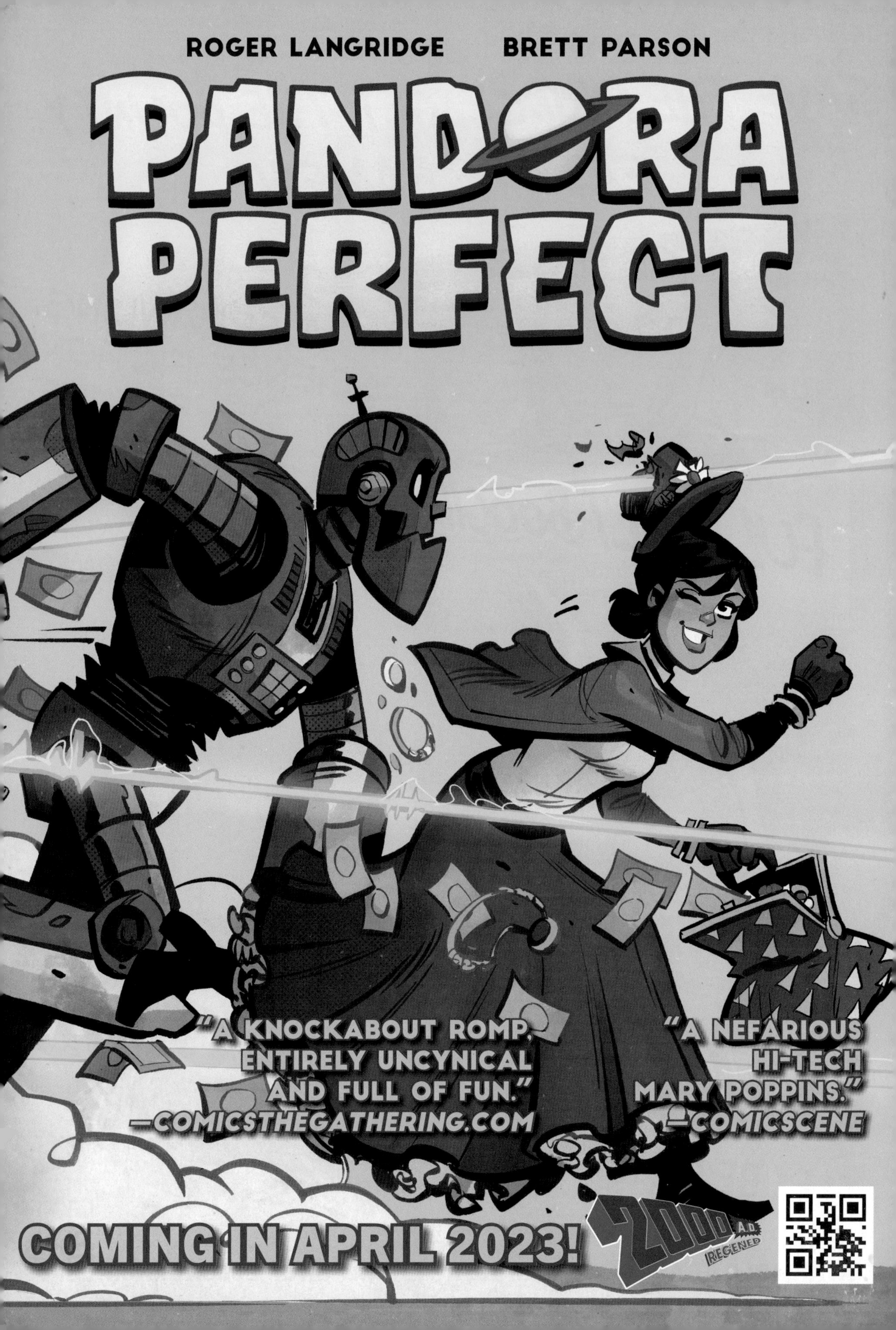
ROGER LANGRIDGE BRETT PARSON
PANDORA PERFECT
"A KNOCKABOUT ROMP, ENTIRELY UNCYNICAL AND FULL OF FUN." —COMICSTHEGATHERING.COM
"A NEFARIOUS HI-TECH MARY POPPINS." —COMICSCENE
COMING IN APRIL 2023!
2000 A.D. REGENED